Bali Blue

An Enemies-to-Lovers Romance

Cher Terais

Aggrandis Group, LLC

Also by Cher Terais

A Wanderlust Romance

Mess on the Mara

Tempest in Tulum

Stay even more connected by scanning the the QR Code below to get bonus content for Cher Terais's books. Discover the fun things like:

The soundtrack to this book and the others

Inspiration boards and visuals for each book;

Free downloadables, short stories and more!

https://linktr.ee/Cher_Terais

The trip doesn't stop here! The Booked Club community and podcast are COMING SOON!

Sign up for my mailing list for all the deets: https://bit.ly/cherteraismailinglist

Bali Blue

An Enemies-to-Lovers Romance

Cher Terais

Aggrandis Group, LLC

Acknowledgements

HERE WE ARE AT the end if this journey called *Bali Blue*. Though my name is solely on its cover, this work of love would not have been possible without the following people.

My daughters, for believing in me and giving me the space to step outside of my role as their mother to embody the characters that take life between these pages.

My family and friends, for all the support and encouragement to hurry and finish this book. Each time y'all asked, "When that book coming out?" was a kick of motivation in my rump!

I'd also like to say thanks to my many followers on Instagram for engaging with me and the content I posted about the characters, settings, and all of what went into this novel. And most importantly for helping me choose the book cover.

I owe special gratitude to Patrick Ahyi-Sena for pushing me and having unwavering faith in my dreams to be a writer, a director, and an all-around *Rich Bitch*. I am forever in your debt. *Literally.* LOL.

Finally, I want to acknowledge the indie authors who write the stories that I love to read about women who look like me, experience the same ups and downs in life as me, and most importantly, you write the stories about us that often go untold. YOU all inspired me to write this book, hopefully the first of many.

In loving memory of my mother. May your spirit live on forever through my pen and characters.

-   We did it, Ree!

Chapter 1 - Rhiyan

J UST AS I WAS about to pack up my computer to leave for the day, Delia, my assistant, poked her head through the crack of my office door. "Stan would like to see you in his office, Rhi," she looked at me with pursed lips and widened eyes like she was nervous on my behalf.

I glanced at her over the reading glasses perched equidistant from the edges of my nose. "Did he mention what he wanted?"

She frantically shook her head sideways, her eyebrows pinched together. "He looks pissed though," she shrugged before turning to walk back to her desk.

It was rare that Stanton Jeffries, my boss, came out of his office, let alone summoned anyone into it. It wasn't that he didn't like people—he was just better at dealing with spreadsheets and numbers than people. Our Monday team meeting was normally the only time we saw him unless one of us was summoned.

"Shit," I muttered under my breath, thinking that I'd be able to skate another week before having to share the status of the Parque

Place project. It was Thursday and *I-be-damned!* It was my turn to be summoned.

I already knew what he wanted. The project budget reports were published by accounting every Thursday morning, and he wanted an update. Better yet, he wanted to rip me a new one regarding the delays on my project Parque Place at the Hamlet, the billion-dollar mixed use development that was currently under construction. The delays were happening under my leadership, and it was time to pay the piper.

The project, which was a flywheel project for 3W, was a big deal and was on the radar of the Atlanta City Council and several other local and state stakeholder groups. The 106-acre property was anchored by a Whole Foods, a dine-in movie theater, and upscale and affordable dining and living perimeters. It was expected to bring a positive economic impact to the area. The media would have a fucking field day with us *screwing the pooch* on this one.

The rooftop community gardens and expansive greenspaces had bike and walking paths, and a state-of-the-art skate park made of reclaimed concrete and used tires. The entire development was built to be environmentally friendly and sustainable. That alone brought in several local investors who wanted to keep Atlanta green. We ran the risk of losing said investors if word of the delays got out.

The goal was to have construction completed on Parque Place before the beginning of the shopping season this year, giving us just under three months to have the buildout complete and tenants—residential and commercial—moving in. It was my job to ensure we met that goal. I had been able to keep the delays under wraps, especially from the media, but numbers didn't lie, and *Budget Man* was pissed.

My feet felt heavy as I trudged across the inlaid marble of the 17th floor office towers of One Ravinia Drive. It was the executive floor of Wiley, Whitman, and White, 3W, an architectural and engineering firm located just outside of Atlanta. I was one of four Executive Vice Presidents and the only black female member of the corporate leadership team. I was certainly not doing my people any favors by being summoned to see the boss today. I was in charge of our commercial business unit, my team being the highest performing team in the company. Did it matter that their fearless leader was present physically every day but absent upstairs? I hoped not.

Stan had a corner office down the hall and around the corner from mine which overlooked Piedmont Park. Not that it mattered. He was too vested in pouring over sales figures, bottom lines, and board meeting notes to ever stop and savor the view. And that was exactly what he was doing when I stepped through the glass doors of his office. There he was—dark hair, super tanned skin, tailored suit—wasting all of that fineness away locked up in a tower at 3W. He was more of a *workaholic* than I used to be. I'm surprised his wife hadn't left him. He was married to the job. She was basically his mistress.

"Stan, good afternoon." I spoke feigning a false bravado as I walked into his expansive, modern office. I extended my hand over his large chrome desk in an act of salutation and respect. He saw right through me.

Cutting to the chase, he nodded to one of the Barcelona chairs with a clipped, "Have a seat, Rhi." His lazy southern drawl was as melodic and lilting as usual, but today held a palpable undertone of frustration.

He continued, "I've been reviewing the financial summary for the Parque Place project, and we are almost two and half million dollars in the red..."

"Two-million," I interjected.

He sat stone-faced on the edge of his seat while staring down at the piece of paper in his hand. "And a full month behind schedule," he said in a matter-of-fact tone. After a heavy silence, he directed his gaze at me and hissed, "What the hell is going on over there?"

"I'm handling..."

"Handling? How?" He broke in, dropping the cool and calm act. "Why are we delayed in the first place?" he started to yell. "You don't seem that on top of it, Rhi! It's our biggest account for crying out loud!"

"I know this is our biggest account!" I countered in irritation while knowing full well that he had every right to question my ability to manage this account. "And I am working with the construction company to make sure we have crews working 24/7 in rotating shifts to get the project back on schedule," I stated, stretching the truth slightly. "When I-85 collapsed, a lot of the materials, including steel beams, rebar, and concrete had to be broken down into smaller lots to be rerouted around the city," I said more confidently and truthfully this time. "All major construction projects across the city are delayed. Not just this one. You know this!" My defensive side finally kicked in.

Flipping the script, I looked at him as if he were the one not performing. He tapped his pen impatiently on his desk, bringing me back to reality. I was out of line. I lowered my voice, "The budget overrun is due to the delays, but our effort to get the construction schedule back on track is working." I hoped he was buying my bullshit. "The project will be completed by late December as planned. Trust me on this," I raised my eyes to his beseechingly.

He gave me a skeptical side-eye before relaxing a bit, "How are we going to recoup the two-million?"

OK. He hadn't bought it. But all BS aside, I *had* worked out a plan to recoup some of the losses and get the schedule back on track.

"Well, we won't be able to recoup all of it up front, but the city of Atlanta is providing a tax incentive to all companies affected by the I-85 collapse. That gives us a shelter of roughly 750k, not sure about the rest, but I have my team trying a few options now."

These were all facts, and he knew it. His intimidating blank stare subsided as he weighed his response. I was a bit unnerved by his silence. Despite the rough patch, my job was everything to me, and I refused to be chastised like some junior flunky.

"Is that all?" I asked sternly, ready to leave. It was getting hard to breath.

He stared at me in silence a little longer, then he sank back into his seat and sighed. He reached up to finger-comb a wayward lock of dark hair away from his forehead, something he often did when he wanted his words to be measured and clear. I saw him do this in the presence of junior associates, but never with me. Our normal banter and interoffice conversations had become quite a bit more strained over time. But this... I wasn't ready for. His words made my shoulders droop.

"Rhiyan, I cannot help but notice that you have been off your game lately. Hell," he paused, taking a deep breath and blowing it out audibly, "the whole office has noticed."

"I know…"

He held up a hand to cut me off.

"Let me finish," his eyes softened before he continued. "I know that you have been hanging by a thread since the divorce," he dropped his voice to an almost whisper. "I get it. Been there before… and even though I'm confident you will get the project back on track, I'm more concerned about *you*."

I wasn't ready for this.

"We cannot afford to lose you, Rhi, but that's where it's headed if you continue to stay stuck on cruise control," his voice trailed off momentarily as I just sat there waiting to see where the conversation was heading. "And though I appreciate that you have a plan to bring Parque Place around, you and I both know the slippages in the schedule could have and should have been taken care of before we went over budget."

I took a deep breath, knowing what he said was true. I dropped my eyes to the floor. In a resigned voice I asked, "Are you firing me?"

"No, Rhi. Haven't you been listening?" he asked, his voice pleading. "We need you, but in better mental shape than you are in now. I think you need to take some time off and get your head together."

My shoulders went rigid. "Time off? What, why?"

"Because you're spiraling," he paused, reining his words in. "If your project is back on track as you say it is and construction will complete by late November on target with our projected goal, take some time off. You need it," he said with a wave of his hand. "Your team can see the project through with your periodic guidance, of course. They...I need you to get your head back in the game, Rhi. If this project goes as planned, next year is gearing up to be our busiest and highest revenue year on record. We *all* need you at your best."

My eyes flashed up from my hands which had been firmly clenched on my lap. I could feel the sharp sting of tears but held them at bay. My performance must have been worse than I thought; his telling me to take some time off felt like an act of pity. My stomach churned in embarrassment from letting my personal life stain my otherwise flawless professional record.

I always prided myself on having my shit together. Top of my class at Northwestern. *Hell*, top of the leaderboard in anything I ever did from academics to tennis.

As if to punctuate his pity, he continued, "You are a valued member of this team. Please take some time and get it together." He may as well have just said: *Girl, get yo' life!*

I took a deep breath and blew it out shakily.

"Yes, Sir." I agreed to check in with my team once a week and spend my two months off immersed in rituals of 'self-care'. Whatever *that* means. The last 10 years of my life revolved around the chaos of my corporate life and my marriage. The two made up my total existence and now… My fucking life was in shambles and *I hate it here.*

I grabbed my notebook before spinning on my heel and walking out, determined to head to my office to grab the rest of my things. I did not grant myself enough time to sulk or feign a farewell. I scanned the room that had been my second home for so long and decided to grab my laptop and the cactus plant that had been drying out on my desk.

I was going to miss my daily chats with Delia. She tried her best to cheer me up by regaling me with her latest escapades of online dating. It did work a little. I secretly admired her *seize the day* attitude, along with her openness and candor about her fucked up yet wickedly funny dating life. Admittingly, her stories took my mind off my own bullshit. Sometimes we'd laugh so hard at all the dates that had gone wrong. Other times, I'd look at her in abject horror. Often sounding like an older sister. "You better be practicing safe sex!" I would warn. I sped up my packing because I didn't want to face her questioning eyes as I prepared to leave the building.

I made it to the parking garage almost unseen aside from the security guard.

"Have a good evening, Ms. Carson."

"You too, Bobby," I called over my shoulder as I slid a pair of YSL sunglasses on my face before stepping out into the sunny upper roof parking deck.

I took a last glance back over my shoulder, taking in the richly appointed lobby of 3W and walked out into the sunshine before a lonely tear drop escaped underneath my shades, betraying the emotion I had worked so hard over the last year to keep at bay. At least at work.

The steady *click-clack* of my Prada heels sounded like the staccato of army drums just before a 21-gun salute as I took deliberate, yet steady strides across the concrete. Jai's voice lilting in my head, "Bitch, stand your ass up straight and strut. You are intrepid."

Intrepid. I smiled woefully through my tears thinking about Jai. She definitely would have used the word *intrepid* in a sultry, drawn out, deep southern drawl. The thought of her kept me from crumbling into a crying wet heap right there in the parking deck.

Chapter 2 - Rhiyan

I SLID INTO THE cockpit of my two-year-old Audi Q5 SUV, barely noticing how the soft leather hugged my curves. I absently tossed my phone onto the wide center console, pushed the start button, and fastened my seatbelt. The supercharged six-cylinder monster roared to life. I used to feel a jolt of exhilaration through my entire body when this beast revved beneath me. At this point, I barely even noticed it. I stopped noticing it after my divorce.

The Bang and Olufsen sound system that I used to play loud and funky eclectic jazz and neo-soul was now constantly playing CNN or NPR radio to provide a form of white noise for my constantly swirling thoughts. My rides home from work were usually filled with that white noise and with me subconsciously trying to make sense of my divorce. However, today, the conversation with Stan played on repeat in my head as I pulled out of the parking garage onto One Ravinia Drive on my way to I-285 W.

What the hell am I going to do now? My job was the only thing keeping me slightly together. Now *this. What am I supposed to do with all this time off?*

"Fuck!" I yelled, striking the steering wheel with the palm of my hand, hitting it hard enough to blow the horn, scaring myself half to death and—no doubt—other folks on the road. The loud noise did serve to snap me out of my reverie enough to refocus on driving. I sat up straighter out of sheer embarrassment, glad my windows were tinted and no one could see my self-pitying tantrum.

"Get it together, Rhi," I said aloud, much calmer this time, wiping the tears from my face with the back of my hand.

Just before driving the last few blocks home, I decided to stop at Bombay Bites, a nearby Indian restaurant, to pick up a small appetizer of Samosa Chat and a large portion of lamb Rogan Josh so I wouldn't have to leave my apartment for at least two days. It didn't take long to get my to-go order, and moments later I was making the final left onto North Peachtree Street NW. *Home.*

"Hi, Ms. Carson!" Norman the doorman stated cheerily as he patted my elbow to help me out of my SUV. "Looking good as always." He kept his hand in place as he walked me around to the entrance of my building. I was glad that I still had on shades so he couldn't see my red-rimmed eyes. I bent down to give him a daughterly kiss on his slightly calloused brown cheek.

His caring mannerisms reminded me of my father, and I believed they were roughly the same age, but that is where their similarities ended. Norman was a shorter, rounder, lighter-skinned black man, hovering around five feet tall. My father, on the other hand, was also in his mid-60s, but tall and lean with a runner's athletic build, a square jawline, and obsidian black skin with a red undertone that made him shine like a new penny. My sister, Jai, had the same athletic build as my father and the same copper brown, butter-smooth skin tone.

I inherited his red-undertone and height, but got everything else from my mother, including her toasted-caramel complexion and wide hips. I'd love to say that my ample ass came from her too, but in truth, my gym-less year was really the blame for that. My mother used to call me 'Redbone' when I was younger. By the time I was in high school and considered myself slightly conscious—*woke* as my niece and nephew would say. I hated when she called me that. I guess one could argue, however, that Mama's reference to my fiery red skin was fairly accurate.

Just like Dad, Norman was always ready to help his 'Baby Cakes'. He had taken to calling me that like my father did. I choked on a laugh as I imagined the nasty, down-the-nose glare my dad would give the man if he ever heard him calling me that. I waved goodbye to Norman as I rounded the corner towards the elevators, where I inserted my special code that allowed access to the 23rd

floor. My 1,600 square feet, overpriced, two-bedroom corner unit overlooking the Federal Reserve Bank of Atlanta and the historic Margaret Mitchell House.

It was an interior designer's dream space. Even though I had decked it out in true showpiece fashion, it served no other purpose than a box where I kept clothes, shoes, and purses that no longer excited me. I guess the one perk was the huge wine rack that I kept stocked with bottles of red wine.

A home, it was not.

I entered the marble foyer, reset the alarm, and took off my heels, placing them in the coat closet along with the other severely pointed, dangerously tall torture devices that screamed 'take me off now' as soon as I crossed the threshold of my front door. I replaced them with my favorite pair of worn-out, furry house shoes to avoid having to walk barefoot on the cold marble and wooden floors.

I continued through the foyer past the floor length pewter-framed mirror, barely noticing my reflection. I walked on to the island in the kitchen, where I laid down my clutch, computer bag, and cell phone before continuing around the corner into the spacious master suite and walk-in closet to take off my black pencil skirt. I gently untied my buttoned lantern-sleeve, jade-green silk top and emerged in a pair of tattered joggers and a Northwestern T-shirt sans bra.

I walked back into the kitchen and sat on my normal perch, a stool at the open end of the long granite waterfall island. It's where I sat every night, watching CNN or aimlessly channel surfing with a long-stemmed glass of Opus One. At almost $400 a bottle, my expensive clothing and shoe fetish had been replaced by a solitary penchant for expensive red wine.

Per usual, I grabbed the remote to turn on CNN and pulled the bag of takeout closer to wrestle with the top of the hot, airtight plastic container of Rogan Josh.

"Damn it," I cursed out loud, sucking my sore fingernail that almost broke off in my efforts to open the tightly sealed plastic food container. "Why is this shit always so hard to open?" I groaned, sucking my finger to ease the throbbing of my nail. Lady Luck must have taken pity on me as the top finally loosened and I avoided dousing my lap in the stewed curry sauce.

I pulled out the Styrofoam cup of rice and spooned the spicy chunks of lamb over it, half listening to the background noise of the TV until a CNN Breaking News alert played over the surround sound. Wolf Blitzer's voice got my attention.

"The popular tourist islands of Bali and Lombok were struck by a 6.9-magnitude earthquake overnight. According to Indonesia's National Disaster Management Agency, Lombok was the epicenter of the quake and sustained the most damage. More than 91 people are reported dead and scores more are reported missing or injured. Hundreds of hikers were left stranded on Mount Rinjani," he said while a video feed of the damage began to play. "We have a video sent by one of the hikers at the summit. This video shows the terrifying moments after the earthquake hit..."

I watched transfixed by the television as additional reports of the earthquake came in.

Chapter 3 - Rhiyan

I WOKE UP WITH the report of the earthquake still fresh on my mind. During Wolf's reporting last night, they showed a haunting still image of a little girl with huge almond-shaped eyes. She was covered in soot and blood. The emotion and tears in her eyes magnified the trauma on her face. It was contorted in anguish as she reached over the shoulder of the rescue worker carrying her to safety. Blackened tears streaked her cheeks as she hysterically reached towards the remains of a small concrete home that he'd pulled her from.

I was sitting at the small desk in my bedroom, nervously waiting for all hell to break loose after hitting send on the Facebook post I crafted with hands that seemed to be guided by a divine spirit. I sat back awaiting the call I knew was coming in 3...2...1.

And just like that, my phone danced across the desk to the hum of Verizon's *Airwaves* ringtone. The inevitable conversation had my tense shoulders squared and ready for battle. I knew I was about to get cursed out. My sister's smiling face and number was plastered on the six-inch gorilla glass phone screen. I was 100% sure that the smile on that photo was not present on her face at the moment.

Deep breath in, slow exhale out. "Hello."

"Bitch, where you supposed to be going without telling me and what is this Facebook message all about?"

I could tell Jai was at work by the way she was whisper-yelling at me, trying to keep her nosy co-workers from hearing our conversation. I'm sure they did anyway. Even though she was a successful marketing exec, she had a flare for the extra. They all knew she was *sophista-ratchet* and were probably tipping their ears up to hear her latest drama-filled conversation.

In a monotone voice, I responded, "I'm sure you read the post, Jai. Why else would you be calling here yelling?"

"Girl, ain't nobody yelling at you!" she yelled, code-switching and turning up on me. "Yes, I did read ya lil' post and I'm trying to figure out when the fuck you planned to take your ass to Java? How you even know that I'm going to be able to take off..."

I promptly cut her off before she got comfortable with the idea that she was invited. "Jai, if you read the message, then you know that I'm going by myself. You're not invi-"

"What the hell do you mean I'm not invited? Who are you going with, then?"

"Girl, what part of #solotravel did you not understand?"

"Rhiyan! You are absolutely not going to Jav-"

"Bali," I corrected her coolly.

"Whatever!" she hissed in frustration. "You are not going anywhere in Indonesia by ya damn self!" she continued. "Don't you watch CNN? There was a 7.0 earthquake there last night."

Her whisper-yelling was much louder now.

Jai'Elle, 'Jai', was my older sister and I respected her as such, but I was not going to allow her to dictate what my grown ass was or was not going to do. *Not today.* I didn't want to hurt her feelings, but this was something I had to do. Don't know why I had to go there, but I knew I didn't need her permission to follow this feeling to Bali.

I steadied and softened my voice.

"Jai, I know you are concerned and slick jealous that I'm going on a trip around the world by myself. I just need to get away from it all. Get to know *me* again." *Self-care,* I thought to myself before continuing. "Work is fucked up. I'm not sleeping. I feel stressed and anxious *all* the time. I just need a..." my voice trailed off as I tried to find the words to get her to understand, before rushing to finish my sentence. "I need a *'Eat Pray Love'* Solange *'Cranes in the Sky'* moment for myself..."

I hoped she would catch my meaning. When she remained silent, I quietly added, "Plus, this way I can spend a little time doing something I love and help out by volunteering in the aftermath

of the quake. I've already checked and much of Bali is unaffected.
That's where I will be staying. See? Safe as can be."

"*Mmm*," Jai mumbled skeptically.

"Yes. I plan to take a boat over to Lombok and maybe some of
the outlying islands to volunteer some of my time in the hospitals
or helping out with displaced children."

"Aww, babe," she said, voice softening a bit.

I could tell that she was still irritated but understood where I was
coming from. Jai was sensitive like that—always willing to take on
my pain and fix it. This time she couldn't fix it. Couldn't fix me.
I needed an escape. Needed to run away. Just like I did from my
bullshit marriage. I ran so fast and furiously, leaving that bastard,
Kyle, to his cheating ass ways. I ran so quickly and absolutely that
I didn't realize a part of my soul got left behind in my mad dash to
freedom.

Jai had been my rock during that time and helped me cry, cuss,
and fight my way to some semblance of recovery after my divorce
last year.

We were both Carson women. Strong, successful, and indepen-
dent. Expected to dust ourselves off, adjust our crowns, and keep it
pushing. Well, I must have also left my crown and greatness in the
rubble of my marriage because I was neither acting queenly nor
great—at work or at home. I couldn't seem to dust myself off or
shake the heartache I was dealing with. I put on a good front, or so

I thought. I now knew my proverbial slip was showing, and I was going to have to do something drastic to get my mediocre, dusty ass life together. And I was flying all the way to Bali, Indonesia to do it.

Jai knew there was no sense arguing with me. My mind was made up the second I hit send on that post.

"Rhi, please be careful and bitch, I'm still mad you didn't invite me. You better stay your ass on FB Live the whole time you're there, so I know where you are and who you're with at all times! Black ass come up missing, don't expect me to come and find you!"

"Will you shut up, Ms. Extra?" I giggled. "Just tell me you will miss me and text me a list of souvenirs you want."

"Hell yeah! It's already on the way," she sighed. "For real though," she finally stopped to take a breath, "I know this year hasn't been easy on you. Please, please, please be safe and let's do happy hour before you go. When you leaving?"

"Monday," I said in a whisper.

"Monday, Rhi!" she full on yelled this time before gathering herself. "Damn. So much for happy hour, bitch."

I loved how she was always fussing over me. Just like Ma used to do before she passed away six years ago.

We wrapped up our call, and I promised to keep her posted on my travel arrangements. Before disconnecting Jai said, "You better call Daddy and let him know about this foolishness. You know he is going to have a fit when he finds out his Baby Cakes is off in some strange land by herself," she chided. "And I'm not doing your dirty work for you."

I could feel sarcasm dripping off her tongue and could see the subsequent eye roll through the phone. I was the youngest and Daddy's little girl; she was just as jealous as I used to be over how close she was to Mom.

I promised that I would and mimicking her tone, I teasingly said, "Bye, bitch. Love you. Call you later."

I reached toward the phone screen to disconnect our call but heard Jai trying to hold my attention.

"Hey, hey, hey," she yelled. "Before I let you go, make sure you find a pretty Asian dick to bounce on over there."

"Girl, what?" I laughed in disbelief at her silly self.

"Chiii," she said in her classic long, drawn-out way. "I heard them little men be on some ol' freaky, tantric shit." I closed my eyes and rubbed my temples because I knew she was about to spew some foolishness out of her lips.

And true to Jai form, she continued, "While you're there, Rhi, might as well let somebody eat, pray, and love on that dusty cooch of yours!" I burst out laughing for the second time in what seemed like ages as she kept on, "Try some tantric shit." At that I hung up on her before she could say anything else.

Honestly, a dick, attached to a man that is, was the last thing I wanted. *Tantric shit.* I was still laughing on the inside. Like who needed some 200-pound man-child sucking the life out of you? After Kyle, I don't think I'd ever trust another man.

Chapter 4 - Kendrick

RING, RING, RING.

I heard the shrill ringing of my cell through a fog of deep sleep. I rolled towards the nightstand, stifling an inward groan as I grabbed it, intent on silencing the ringing. Still drenched in sleep, I attempted to hit the decline button, but my clumsy fingers somehow missed that one altogether, and I ended up answering the damn thing.

I took a deep, calming breath to quell the desire to rip into whoever was on the other line. Especially if it was the chick from the other night. She seemed like the type who wouldn't get the hint and would want to turn a casual one-nighter into something more. I thought I had made it clear that I didn't play that pop-up or 'booty call in the middle of the night' shit. Not when I was on full daddy duty. It was a school night.

Half hoping, half dreading that it was Jade calling, I warily glanced at the brightly lit display. My tightened chest relaxed then immediately tensed again at the unrecognized international number. This couldn't be good. I also ruled Jade out. I felt a wave of relief only because no call from her at this hour was a good sign. Then, I was pissed all over again. *Who the fuck is calling me at 4 a.m.?*

I jerked my body over onto my back and let my head fall forcefully onto the pillow. Blowing out an audible breath, I answered, "You better have a damn good reason for calling me at this hour."

"Kendrick," I heard a familiar voice say through the phone. "It's Ketut," his voice going in and out over the static of the line.

I bolted up straight in the bed, clutching the phone tighter and pressing it more firmly to my ear.

"Ketut?" I asked, clearing the remaining cobwebs from my brain. "I can hardly hear you. What's going on?"

"Kendrick, there's been an earthquake... pretty bad. Lots of damage," more static, "way worse than the last time. Damage to roads, buildings..." His words trailed as another wave of static drowned him out.

While waiting for the line to clear enough for me to understand him again, I fished the remote off the nightstand to turn on the news. I keyed the numbers in for CNN International and there it was. The headline read: '7.0 Earthquake Causes Severe Damage to Parts of Bali and Surrounding Islands.' I sat there glued to the images of destruction that flashed like a carousel across the screen.

"…We are going to need help here with the reconstruction," Ketut's voice came back in, this time loud and clear. "I need you to come. We don't have the resources to lead a major rebuild."

"What about equipment?" I asked, jumping straight into CEO mode.

"Equipment? Yes, yes. We have heavy equipment and everything you told us to get after the last quake. Just need a team that can get this done quick."

"Say less," I said, now fully alert.

I swung my legs over to the side of the bed and grabbed the nape of my neck. I squeezed and released, then massaged the tight muscles to release some of the tension that had been slowly building since the damn phone started ringing. I had been fully prepared to curse Jade's ass out for going ghost again, knowing damn well Jada, our daughter and the only good thing that came out of our union, needed her mother right now more so than me.

Our baby girl, tomboy that she was, should have been preparing for her middle school cheerleading tryouts, but was too busy trying to break her neck learning new tricks on that damn skateboard I mistakenly bought. And Jade had been MIA for the last week. Most likely on another binger.

I hadn't expected the call to be from Ketut. We'd talked a few times over the last two years, but with all of the recent and extreme weather systems, hurricanes, earthquakes, and more frequently now, wildfires, my team of civil and structural engineers had been stretched to the limit. Wherever a natural disaster hit, Kekoa Industries was there; we specialized in infrastructure rebuild. And we would be there to lead the effort Ketut was asking for.

Images of a younger Ketut crossed my mind. The distress in his voice now, brought back eerie memories of another time, many years ago when the same distress was present. Back then, he carried the distress from an all-too-similar disaster in his swollen, red eyes. A memory that I should have been too young to have but it came rushing back all the same.

"Give me a few days to get Jada situated, then me and a small crew will be on the next thing smoking."

We exchanged a few more words; he provided details of where to fly into since the main airport runway was decimated. I reassured him that we'd be there as soon as humanly possible.

I knew I wouldn't be able to get much sleep after my call with Ketut. I opted to go downstairs and hit the weights to relieve the tension. Jada would be up soon anyway to get ready for school and I needed some time to think about what excuse I was going to tell her about why her mom didn't show up for her surf competition yesterday.

I got Jada off to school without a hitch but did let her know that I had a job coming up out of town and that she'd have to stay with

TiTi Ona for a little while. Jade, her mom, just wasn't dependable but it was not something I had the heart to say to her.

Being the happy-go-lucky girl she always was, she bounced out of the car, blew me a kiss, and yelled, "Don't worry, Dad. You know I love staying with TiTi. She knows things!" she said, pointing her index finger comically at her temple.

"And what does TiTi Ona know that I don't?" I asked, a wounded yet playful look on my face. Jada shot me a side-eye and a smirk as if to say, 'None of your business.' I chuckled, gesturing with my pointer and index finger from my eyes to hers, "I'm watching you and Ona's crabby ass, young lady."

"You should be," she giggled and closed the door running off towards a group of her friends. I loved that kid to death. She and my Auntie Ona were as thick as thieves and did everything together. It always amazed me that Ona could keep up with Jada even in her 70s and showed no sign of slowing down. I decided to make her house my next stop.

I pulled up to Ona's modest home and poked my head in to call out her name. I knew if she didn't answer she would be in the back drinking a cup of coffee, smoking a cigarette, and watching the fisherman busying themselves with morning activities, cleaning and sorting the fish they caught to sell at the market. It was a blessing that Jada had a female figure like Ona in her life.

She was exactly where I knew she'd be. With her long silky grey hair hanging loose down her back, she looked angelic and peaceful sitting out there on the porch. Looks were deceiving. Ona was feisty and would give the devil a run for his money. An angel wouldn't stand a chance.

"Those nasty things are going to kill you," I said, walking up behind her to give her a big bear hug, almost knocking the ashtray off her small lap.

"Get your meat hooks off me, *kane*!" she hissed in her gravelly broken English and Pidgin calling me a boy. "Where the hell was ya' and that no-good mama of Jada's yesterday when that baby was giving it all she had out on dem waves?"

I took a step back as Ona rounded on me as if to deck me in the nose.

"Alright now! Watch it, old lady!" I jumped back, dodging her tiny fist. "Watch where you're swinging those little jumper cables before you hit one of these lava rocks and hurt yourself!" I warned, laughing before flexing my pecks up and down.

At that, she threw her head back in a deep, throaty laugh before saying, "You better *nuh* hurt your damn self, Kendrick."

Sobering up, she said, "Jada, know you *nuh guh* be there because you had work. She *nuh* say, but I could tell *dah* she hurt that her mama *nuh* there!"

I nodded in agreement with my aunt, feeling bad because I could tell Jada was in a funky mood yesterday when I picked her up. I solemnly added, "Yeah, I know she was hurt. After I picked her up, she took her shower and went straight up to her room. I just let her be." I raised my shoulders in a shrug. I wasn't going to continue to make excuses for Jade. I wasn't going to bad-talk her to Jada, but my baby girl was being let down.

As if realizing how early it was for the first time, Ona cocked an inquisitive brow at me before narrowing her eyes.

"What *dah* bitch do now?"

I cocked my head to the side meeting her glare, taken off guard by her abrupt change. Then it dawned on me that she thought I was here so early because Jade had done something to Jada.

"I honestly don't know where Jade is. She hasn't been around in over a week. That's not what I'm here for."

Ona's face softened, "*Hmph*... it must be something *guh* on. You never come by this early unless something *guh* on at work or *wih* Jade."

"Work," I stated definitively.

"Where *fo* now, Kendrick?"

"Bali. Ketut called."

Not remembering the name, she questioned me with her eyes.

"Ketut, Minister of the Interior of Bali. There was an earthquake there last night. They need a team."

Before I could finish Ona was already nodding, "No *boddah*. She be fine. We need *fo* finish *da* birdhouse we make anyway. How long you *guh* be gone?"

"It's pretty significant damage, Auntie. Might be there for a month."

Not showing any concern, "Oh *ya*! Me and baby girl *guh* get into lots of trouble while you gone," Ona chuckled.

I groaned knowing that I was probably going to come home to Jada throwing up gang signs after spending so much time with my thug-ass auntie. Ona was my aunt on my dad's side of the family, but instead you'd think she was from my mom's side from Bed-Stuy in Brooklyn. She was hardcore half the time but as sweet as pie when I needed her to be and with Jada.

I prepared to leave and leaned in to plant a kiss on Ona's forehead. She caught my face in her hands before pinching and patting my cheek. "How *bah* you get *fo* some trouble too while you're out galivanting across *da* world?" she teased, her eyes still gleaming with humor. "Maybe you find a nice *wahine fo* move to Hawaii *fo* be you wife!" she cackled as I threw my head back in disbelief at the words coming out of her mouth. "Maybe you stop trying *fo* fix *dah* broken bird of woman, Jade."

I dropped my head in exasperation.

"Bye, Auntie. Thank you for always being there for me and Jada."

I left after that to head to the office.

Chapter 5 – Rhiyan

I SAT AT GATE 31 on Concourse A in the south terminal fidgeting through the contents of my carryon bag for the umpteenth time, checking and rechecking its contents as I waited to board Delta flight 1594 to LAX.

I couldn't sleep the night before, so I was up at the crack of dawn. I had already packed my bags over the weekend, so I had nothing but time on my hands as I waited for my 6 p.m. departure. I called an Uber around 3 to take me to the airport because I knew sitting at home waiting would only open the door to self-doubt. I'd be making every excuse in the book on why this trip was such a big mistake. Better yet, I'd probably be fretting over silly things like whether I packed enough panties or not. I'd keep checking and rechecking my bags to ensure I packed toothpaste, as if they only sold these things in the U.S.

It was still an hour until boarding time, and I had been sitting in the terminal long enough to memorize Mayor Keisha Lance Bottom's address to travelers coming in and out of Hartsfield-Jackson.

I'd subconsciously focused my attention on the sound of her voice and the hustle and bustle of the airport in an effort to stop stewing over this forced time off. The mayor's address was playing now over the loudspeaker for the umpteenth time, and I unconsciously recited it along with her in my head.

"...Hello, I'm Mayor Keisha Lance Bottoms. Welcome to Harts-field Jackson, Atlanta's International Airport. Whether Atlanta is your home or you are visiting for business or leisure...yada, yada, yada..."

As many times as I had flown in and out of this airport for work, I never paid much attention to the announcement before. Yet now that I thought about it, I believed they were the exact same words spoken by Mayor Kasim Reid, our previous mayor.

"Damn, as much money as this airport makes for Fulton and the surrounding counties, she couldn't come up with anything original? The only difference was the voice and the name," I mumbled to myself.

As other flight information played over the speaker system, I kept busy by observing the passersby. In that sense, the airport was nothing short of entertaining. You might see anything—from a person arguing with themselves to another setting up a tip cup to serenade the crowds in hopes of making some money. Today, we were all being entertained by a young lady doing a terrible rendition of Beyonce's *Halo*.

I was glad to turn my attention from that hot mess to the harassed young mother yanking her wayward son down the concourse with one hand while balancing a small baby against her opposite hip with her other arm. I could tell she was about two seconds from popping him on the behind for not hurrying up.

A business traveler in gray slacks and blue sports jacket was pecking away with one hand on his Surface Pro while talking loudly on his cell phone. He was holding the speaker of his wired headset to his lips so the listener could hear him a little better over the continuous loud flight announcements. I couldn't help but wonder if the person on the other end was hard of hearing because I could hear their whole conversation from six rows away.

And so, it went. I continued to find anything to focus on rather than the fact that I was flying halfway around the world in search of... I don't know what. A part of me hoped all of this was for something.

As we got closer to boarding, I could feel my anxiety growing. I refocused on the present activities of the airport again to keep my nerves at bay. The gate began to fill up with various travelers all headed to LAX. Several people were lined up at the flight desk trying to get seat upgrades or get rebooked on this flight or another. The gate agent was visibly irritated and made no qualms about letting it show either.

Outside the wall of windows, I could see several airplanes, all with the red and blue signature colors of Delta on their tails. They were lined up neatly in a long row one after the other and catty-cornered to the lowered jet bridges. I was impressed by the efficiency of it all as they worked incessantly to get the luggage, food, and beverages loaded onto each airplane.

Anxiety palpable at this point, I had to take a few deep, steadying breaths. *Why the fuck did I plan a trip to a place that just had an earthquake? What if Jai was right? I didn't have any business going to a foreign country by myself.* A few more deep breaths.

I squeezed my eyes shut for a minute in silent meditation in the last few minutes before my departure time. The nervousness was starting to subside, and my breathing was much easier.

The loudspeaker jumped back to staticky life, and I slowly opened my eyes as the announcement began to play. "In five minutes, we will begin the pre-boarding process on Delta Flight 1954 to LAX…"

I settled into my seat in first class, still having second thoughts about this whole thing of flying off to Bali to 'find myself' but was again snapped out of my thoughts from a tap on my shoulder.

"Pardon me, I'm next to the window."

My seat mate, a beautiful light-skinned sister with braids hanging down to her waist, inched past me to take her seat. She had shells interwoven into a few of them, giving her a very tribal vibe. I looked over at her and smiled.

"Hi, how's it going?" I asked politely.

She gave me a tired half smile before saying, "Good and tired. Ready to be wheels up so I can go to sleep."

I tipped the glass of red wine the waitress had brought me moments earlier. "Cheers to that," I said in agreement.

Sounded like music to my ears. I wasn't in much of a chatty mood with a stranger on a plane while contemplating life-changing moves. I didn't feel like answering the dreaded questions sure to come. *Where are you headed? Business or pleasure? You traveling alone?* The last question made me the most nervous. I mean what would I say? I could lie and say I was meeting a lover in the Island of the Gods. Or I could just not answer, but that would be rude. Saying the truth was not an option.

With a thin-lipped smile and a nod, she put on her headphones, closed her eyes and was out before the external doors of the plane were closed. I put on my headphones, following suit and five minutes later, we were airborne.

A couple hours into the flight, I opened my eyes, not realizing I had dozed off too. I looked over at my seat mate to find her pecking away at her laptop with a glass of red wine in hand. *My girl...* She saw that I was awake and mouthed something to me. Not being a lip reader, I had to pull the right earbud out of my ear, holding it up so she could see why I was looking at her dumbfounded.

She repeated, "Heading home?"

"No, Atlanta is home. I'm on my way to Bali. LAX is a layover. How about you?"

"On my way to LAX for business," she replied.

"Ok. Nice. Is Atlanta home for you?"

"No, not anymore. Used to be, but I moved to Kenya two years ago. Flew through Atlanta to handle some business before heading out to LA. You traveling to Bali alone?"

And there it was… the dreaded question I knew was sure to come. Before responding I gave her a discerning look, appraising this woman that I barely knew to see if I could detect any judgment or pity in her eyes. She seemed innocent.

"Yes." The single word lingered in the space between us.

"Oh, that's what's up! You must be one of them 'Sisters Traveling Solo'?" she asked, using air quotes.

I didn't have a clue what she was talking about. Hell, I was still wrapping my head around the fact that this sister lived in Kenya.

"I'm sorry," I stated shaking my head slightly. "What is 'Sisters Traveling Solo'? And did you say you live in Kenya? Like Mother Africa, Kenya?"

Chuckling and rolling her eyes at me as if I were slightly slow, she said, "Yes girl, Kenya as in Mother Africa, Kenya. You can't imagine the looks I get when I say that to people."

"Well, around these here parts," I said in my best southern dialect. "We see a lot of Africans converted to ATL-iens but I don't think I've met a single soul before you from ATL who moved to Africa." We both laughed.

"Hell, me either," she responded. Sobering up, I placed a finger to the dimple of my cheek in contemplative thought. "It's sort of like a reverse diaspora, right?"

She considered the question before responding through twisted lips and a side-eye in my direction. "On first thought, that might be the dumbest shit I ever heard. But yeah. I guess it is a reverse diaspora." It took me a few seconds to pick up on her joke, but then I burst out laughing so hard.

She was laughing just as hard as she struggled to say, "Girl, I thought you was 'bout to slap the shit out my smart-mouthed ass! The look on your face was priceless."

"*Chiii,* for a second I was. Like no this *bih* didn't!" I put my right hand in the air signaling a high five, finishing with a friendly, "Girl, you good." We slapped palms and continued to share a sister-bonding moment. Shit, I was impressed.

After a while she said, "Since I have been in Kenya, I travel around the continent as much as I can. On a recent trip to the west side," she laughed at her own joke as she threw up both hands in the universal sign for *west-side*, "I ran into a group of sisters from the States. They all had on these T-shirts that said 'Sisters Traveling Solo' on them. After seeing a few other groups with the same shirts on, I had to ask one of them what it meant. The sister was proud to share that they were a group of black women, not all of them, who travel around the world solo, and they wore these shirts so they could recognize each other."

"Interesting," I said. My curious stare spurred her on.

"So, naturally, when you said you are traveling alone to Bali, I assumed you were part of this group. From what I hear, they have a huge Facebook community of about 60,000 women of color who are dedicated to debunking the myth that we don't travel. I'm thinking about joining myself."

I looked at her with brows raised, surprised to hear about such a group.

"I wish I had heard of this group while I was preparing for this trip," I let it slip, not sure if I wanted to give up any more details about my solo trip. I just left it right there, and she didn't press any further.

Humph, if anybody else asked me if I was traveling solo, I was going to say, 'Yep. Sure am. I am a Sister Traveling Solo and point them to the Facebook page'. Little white lie... but *who was gon' check me?* I genuinely smiled from the inside out, something that seemed to be happening more and more since booking this trip.

We continued our small talk for the remainder of the flight and parted ways after landing in LA. I sat in the Delta Sky Club for the remainder of my layover in LAX and reflected on the conversation I had with my seatmate from the last flight. Her name was Andra. We shared FB contact information to stay in touch. She was an executive chef who specialized in vegan dishes and had decided to move to Kenya to take her healthy lifestyle and vegan brand to the country. It turned out that she and her business partner were also starting a Kenyan/safari-themed restaurant in Atlanta; the business she mentioned handling during our flight.

She was headed to LA to garner a deal for a cookbook and a reality-based lifestyle show focused on healthy living that would be broadcasted on the Kenyan equivalent of the Cooking Network. Shit, her story was impressive, and I was certainly rooting for her. I wanted to stay in touch to see how everything would go. Her story certainly inspired me to take charge of my own future and one day, start my own firm.

Furthermore, my conversation with her made me feel a lot better about traveling all the way to Bali by myself. The rest of my trip was fairly uneventful, a lot more relaxed and much less self-conscious.

Chapter 6 - Rhiyan

TWENTY SOMETHING HOURS LATER, including a layover in Sydney, Australia, I touched down in Denpasar, Indonesia. Much to my surprise, Ngurah Rai airport was fairly modern with a well-stocked duty-free shop. It contained perfumes from Marc Jacobs to Givenchy, any beauty product you could find in Sephora and other posh beauty retailers. There were nice restaurants, luxurious shopping boutiques, massage parlors, and more lining the wide shining hallways of the airport. Best of all, the signs pointing to customs and immigration were in Indonesian and English. *Whew.* I was going to be in a world of trouble if they weren't.

Because I'd handled the minimal entry requirements to get into Indonesia before leaving Atlanta, customs and immigration was a breeze. I collected my luggage from claim seven and made my way towards the exit signs. Before leaving, I stopped by an ATM to take out some money. I chose the ATM rather than the money exchanger because I purposefully carried no US dollars, knowing I would be needing Indonesian rupiah. I had also researched the currency and exchange rates before booking my flight. I was surprised to see that the minimum note I could take from the ATM machine was 50,000 rupiah and the maximum withdrawal amount was 2,500,000 rupiah.

I laughed at myself as I remembered the exchange rate. Two and a half million rupiah equated to roughly $175. I was rich by no stretch of the imagination. Stashing the cash in my crossbody, I was on my way.

I stepped out of the cool airport onto the ground transportation curb and was dashed by a hot bucket of steaming air. *Whoa*. Nothing I read about Bali prepared me for this heat and humidity. I guess I should have known better. It was considered to be rainforest. Still, I wasn't ready.

After getting past the rush of heat that slapped me, I was next overwhelmed by the rushing crowd of people dashing out of the airport doors trying to find their waiting taxis and transport. I was even more overwhelmed by the sea of yelling drivers shoving signs with different names in my face as they were looking for their passengers. *How the fuck am I supposed to find my ride in this mob?*

After standing still and trying to adjust my eyes to read the small writing on all of the small pieces of paper being waved around, I saw my name attached to a poster on a stick high above the crowd. By His traveling mercy, I had the smartest driver of them all. Even though my name was spelled all kinds of wrong, I made out Ree-Anne Carson with no problem. I walked hurriedly over to the driver holding my name on a stick and scared the mess out of him when he looked up to find me towering over him.

"Hi, I am Rhiyan Carson. I think you are my driver."

He shifted his eyes around me to see if I was alone. Upon spotting no one else, he said, "Yes. Yes, *Mum*. Please let me *took yours* bag. Are you *travels* alone?"

It took me a minute to understand him through his thick accent, but I eventually caught on and this time, I shrugged and waved off the question with a flick of my wrist. I smiled and looked him square in the eye and said, "Yes. Yes I am." Opting against adding the bit about being a *Sister Traveling Solo.*

"Very *goods*, *Mum*," he nodded smartly. "Follow me."

He grabbed my bags and quickly jetted through the throng of drivers and passengers in the direction of the parking deck. I tried to keep up, but my way was blocked by the mob. He doubled back, grabbed my wrist, and whisked us through the crowd, making light work of the path to the taxi stands.

Away from the crowds, he asked, "First *times* to Bali, *Mum*?"

"Yes," I stated, still trying to catch my breath.

By the time we reached the car, my face was slick with sweat. This did not go unnoticed by my driver, whose name was Danny. As soon as my bags were settled into the trunk and he took his seat behind the wheel, Danny cranked up the air, handed me a cold bottle of water and a cool cloth to wipe my face. I could have kissed his short ass! Apparently, he was used to foreigners being unprepared for the sweltering heat.

We were pulling out into traffic when I realized the driver's seat was on the right side of the vehicle. And it wasn't until I saw traffic coming straight towards us, that it registered they drive on the left side of the road in Bali. My heart was in my panties the entire ride to the hotel. We sped down the narrow two-lane streets. Danny drove like an expert speed racer, dipping in and out of the other cars and skillfully maneuvering around the gazillion scooters that were dipping in and out of traffic at breakneck speeds, too.

There were obviously no road rules here. As I held on for dear life, I asked, "How often are there wrecks in Bali?"

"Hardly *anys*, *Mum*," Danny smiled. "Well, *onlys* when the Aussies drink too *muchs* down in Jimbaran *afturs* surfing all day. You are safe, *Mum*."

Satisfied with his response, I relaxed enough to take in the beach-lined cityscape that almost looked like a postcard. As we drove south to the beach town of Nusa Dua, the cityscape morphed into lush greenery and beautiful resorts. I had yet to see any of the destruction that I was expecting to see from the earthquake. I never experienced a full-on earthquake in Atlanta. We got a few tremors, but nothing nearly as catastrophic as the earthquakes that were prevalent in this part of the world. Based on the news reports, I was expecting to find toppled buildings and washed-out roads.

"Danny, it doesn't appear that the earthquake did much damage to the island. The way the news outlets were reporting, I expected to see a lot more."

He looked at me through the rearview mirror; despite his wary tone, he still managed to wear a smile, which spoke more to his skills in the tourism industry than his happiness to be driving me around.

"It's no *affects* this area to *muchs*, but still pretty *bads* out in the, *er...*" he paused, trying to find the right word, *"rurals* part and closer to the *norths* in the mountain regions of Renjan."

I detected a hint of sadness in his eyes, but it was quickly masked again before he continued, "Bali's economics is heavy base on *touristings*. Kuta, where we *leaves*," he gestured back towards the airport we'd just left, "is *opens* for business as usual. Other areas too, *Mum*, like Nusa Dua, Jimbaran, Seminyak, the places where the best resorts are such as yours, *not damage* because they were built a bit *betturs*. *Howevers*, where many locals *livings*, still *bads*. No electric. No running waters. But Bali build back *strongs*," he finished, holding up a muscled arm in the rear-view where our eyes locked and he smiled. His optimism was infectious. After a brief pause, he continued in a reassuring tone, "No worries, *Mum...* you have *goods* time in Bali. The nightlife is *goods*. Beaches is *goods* and *beautifuls*. We are used to big quake here. Party no *stops* in Bali."

He assumed I was here on vacation, and I didn't correct him.

Twenty minutes later we rounded a final bend in the road and ran smack dab into an opulent oasis. Just as Danny had explained, it looked virtually untouched by the earthquake.

"Welcome to the Hotel Nikko, Ms. Carson," the waiting staff greeted.

A porter who couldn't have been a day over 16 briskly whisked my luggage out of Danny's open trunk, smiling sheepishly before saying, "Let me take your bags, Ms. Carson."

Another member of the hotel staff handed me a cool towel and sparkling champagne flute of mimosa. I accepted it graciously. All of this and I hadn't even made it to the check-in desk yet. I was thoroughly impressed. I paid Danny a handsome tip and thanked him for getting me here safely. In return, he handed me a slip of paper with his WhatsApp details imploring me to call him if I should need a driver to take me around the island.

The check-in process was a breeze, and my bags were taken to my room while I finished up. The mimosa was a momentarily refreshing treat, but the strong champagne combined with jet lag was beginning to take its toll. I was glad to be on my way to the room. As I walked across the open-air lobby, I could see the crystal blue waters of the Indian Ocean just over the horizon. Tantalizing smells of spicy Balinese food tickled my nose and a few sneezes and steps later, I was standing in front of my room door.

My breath was taken away as I entered the lavishly appointed space. The room was decked out in beautifully laid mahogany wooden floors that shone like polished pennies. The king-sized bed was adorned with an intricately carved piece of wood of a lighter hue than that of the floors but was the perfect balance of harmony against the taupe, jute-covered walls. The pillow top beckoned me, but I was too excited by the beauty of the room to be enticed into its embrace just yet. The white fluffy comforter looked cool to the touch in exact opposition to the sweltering heat outside.

The far end of the room opened to a small balcony flanked by open mahogany pocket doors that could be closed to block the bright light of the sun, but who would want to close off the exquisite beauty just over the horizon of the welcoming balcony? I walked to the opening to get a better view.

The shaded outdoor space was covered in large tiles of Jerusalem stone that wrapped up and over a half wall at the front of the private balcony. The green cushions on the outdoor seating perfectly matched the green of the chaise lounge just inside the space of the room and the teakwood table matched the wood of the desk. It was a beautifully decorated space inside and out.

I made my way out to experience the balcony and marveled at the way the horizon wedded a peaceful, blue sky with greenish hues of the Indian Ocean. The entire resort was perched atop a cliff and meandered downhill to meet at the edge of a private beach. The crashing waves flanked with tropical birds cawing provided the perfect soundscape to the beautiful scene before me.

I briefly closed my eyes, taking in the aroma of honey-suckled frangipani mixed with the salty mist from the crashing waves against the cliffs below. Slightly to my right and nearer to the balcony, I could see the white foam-tipped waves, licking the sands of the beach below. I imagined what it would feel like to dip my face into the rippling softness of that foam. I wondered how it would taste on my lips. As salty as all the tears I wasted?

I turned around, shoulders lowered in surrender, as I took another sweeping look at the interior of the room. I would not find out today how the crystal-clear waters below me would feel or taste because I was quickly losing the battle to the luring call of the bed. I sat first on its edge and ran my hands against the crisp coolness of the white cotton comforter. I inched up towards the center and rested the side of my face against the cool softness of a fluffy pillow.

My last thought before drifting off to sleep was of the sounds and smells of the ocean below. And with a smile on my face, I was swallowed by the welcomed solace of sleep.

Chapter 7 - Rhiyan

J UST AS I HAD imagined almost a week ago, the ocean and the private beach at Hotel Nikko would become my best friends. Aside from the occasional emails and the scheduled weekly meeting with my team, my days were mine to do with as I pleased. I had little use for an alarm clock. Of course, that would all change next week when my volunteer work started at the school and hospital. But for now, I was enjoying the freedom. I was doing 'me' and enjoying the time with myself, falling asleep when I wanted and being awakened by the glittering rising sun each morning. It amazed me how hard it had been for me to get up in the mornings when my alarm went off at 8 a.m. back home, but over here I woke up at 6 a.m. and sometimes earlier by my own internal alarm clock with no problem.

My daily routine of sitting on the amazing patio with a large mug of lemongrass tea, listening to the waves and the birds dancing in the purple, pink, and gold morning light resuscitated me back to life. It became my ritual. Thinking, meditating, and simply enjoying the quiet before the rest of the resort came to life. I was taking full advantage of the solitude of the empty beach in the mornings, sporting the only swimsuit I brought with me.

I stifled a quick chuckle as I thought back to my first morning here and my reluctance to wear this same swimsuit. It took a bit of pep-talking myself in the mirror to put it on, but I pushed past my insecurities.

Jai picked the sexy number out for me last year when we were planning a trip to Jamaica that had fallen through. I had gained a few extra pounds since then and thought the one-piece would cover up all my problematic areas. *Wrong.* I mistakenly never tried the thing on until the morning I got to Bali, and it was a whole '*oh shit*' moment since the suit barely covered my front or rear.

My pep talk was very similar to one of Issa Ray's '*mirror bitch*' moments from her HBO hit series *Insecure.* I literally had to look myself square in the eye and say, "You look just fine, Rhi!" After that, I threw my shoulders back, making a promise to myself to stop caring what anyone thought of me and was out the door headed to the beach. After only a week of being here, I discovered a newfound self-confidence that Kyle had slowly stripped away from me. Maybe this trip was what I needed after all.

This morning, unlike the first, I felt a lot more at ease, carefree, even. I was feeling so good about me that, not only did I dive into the ocean away from the other guests, but I also sashayed up the incline to the pool without wearing a cover up and dove right in. I was spending more time than usual out on the beach. By this time of morning, the pool was packed with other resort dwellers, and I didn't care. I didn't even notice them at all. I only cared about how good the cool water felt against my hot sun-kissed skin. It felt liberating. I smiled as I climbed out of the water and caught a glimpse of a younger woman scouring at her man who was openly gawking at me.

I finished my swim and made it back to my room. I showered before sitting at the foot of the bed wrapped in a large fluffy towel finger-combing my freshly washed coils. I had done the hard work of detangling the thick tresses in the shower while my hair was saturated in my favorite detangling and hydrating conditioner. I made the decision to travel light to Bali, leaving behind a flat iron, curling iron, and blow dryer and solely packing my favorite shampoo, conditioner, and moisturizers to help tame my wild hair.

It had been years since I had a perm, but I had always worn my hair pressed straight—another hang-up I was going to have to let go of. I wore it straight because that's how Kyle loved it. He hated when I rocked my natural hair. I continued to wear it straight out of habit and fear that my natural locks would offend my corporate counterparts. For these reasons, I spent countless Saturdays in the salon trying to get my hair fried, dyed, and laid to the side.

Well, fuck Kyle and fuck societal norms. This was my head, and I was going to wear my hair how I damn well pleased from now on. Plus, no amount of pressing would hold up to this tropical steam bath anyway.

Every day, I was learning more creative ways to style it and I was growing to love its untamed thickness cascading over my shoulders and down my back. So much so, that I was going to wear it wild and free on the sightseeing outing that Danny agreed to take me on today.

I finished getting dressed and prepared to go to the lobby and wait on Danny to pick me up. So far, the only thing I had seen in Bali was the resort, the beach, the pool, Chinese and Australian tourists at the resort, and the Balinese hotel staff. I decided to get out and experience some of the sights Bali had to offer before starting my volunteer mission in a couple of days.

I wondered if there were any other black people here. I was sure there had to be, but I didn't see a single one at the resort I was staying at. I laughed on the inside as I thought, *I hope I see at least one today*.

Like clockwork, Danny was parked out front of the hotel at exactly 2 p.m. As soon as he spotted me, he opened the backseat door, gesturing for me to get in and we were off.

Tourists were everywhere. Most of them appeared to be European or Australian. All were deeply tanned with sun bleached hair revealing the amount of time they were spending on beaches and waves. They all carried surfboards or had them strapped to their scooters as they jetted to the beckoning waves that were clearly visible between the many shops and resorts lining the narrow streets.

We continued on our journey, rounding a steep curve around a rocky wall that jutted up towards the heavens. Perched midways up the rocky cliff there was a sign made of huge letters that read: *Welcome to Padang-Padang Beach*.

My heart had already swelled a bit and my face was aching from the joyous smile that split my lips as Danny said, "This the *fames* Padang-Padang beach *froms* movie *Eat Pray Loves*."

I squealed in delight, clapping like a silly kid, not even having to tell him that the book was one of my favorites and that Bali and the famed Padang-Padang Beach were both on my bucket list because of it. Without even knowing it, Danny was helping me fulfill a dream.

Afterward, we stopped by a coffee plantation where I tried *luwak* coffee. Supposedly, it was considered the most exclusive coffee in the world due to its uncommon method of production. Unfortunately, I didn't fully grasp what that production method entailed until after I tasted it. I didn't know whether I should be upset at Danny for not letting me know, or at the *luwak* farmer who plucked the coffee beans from the civet cats' shit in order to sell it! *Can't believe I allowed Danny to talk me into drinking that shit. Literally... shitty coffee!*

Several hours later and after I chewed enough gum to clear my palate, we sat down to eat spicy noodles from a street vendor. By the time Danny took me back to the resort, I was beat. I knew I would fall fast asleep after taking my evening shower. Before drifting, I smiled as I replayed my day with Danny back through my mind. I had seen another solo black girl seated a few seats down from us as we had lunch in a small *warung* eatery. She sported the black t-shirt with the golden words '*Sisters Traveling Solo*' emblazoned across the front. We caught eyes and shared a knowing look and a warm smile before she disappeared down the street.

I woke up and completed my daily routine but ended up sitting by the beach reading the entire day, enjoying the last bit of down-time I had before meeting with Nugroho at the school tomorrow. I talked with him a few days ago, and we discussed my assignment with the Yayasan Waha Mulia Foundation, better known as YUM. I chose this organization because of its connection with the Clinton Global Initiative, which I worked with in the past on smaller volunteer projects back in Atlanta.

YUM specifically provided health and educational resources to the underprivileged in Indonesia. They committed to sourcing a building and staffing it with volunteers from around the globe to provide normalcy to areas affected by the quake. I was proud to be one of those volunteers and loved the concept of a pop-up, learning and community support center for children ranging in age from 5 to 17.

I would be teaching basic reading skills to the island kids who were displaced after the quake. He reiterated that the parents of many of them had passed away or were badly injured and in the hospital. His organization was responsible for upholding a makeshift education and recreation center to provide some normalcy for these kids as the government worked to rebuild the infrastructure of the island. I couldn't wait to jump in and help out in any way I could.

Chapter 8 - Rhiyan

WHEN I ARRIVED AT the school, I was quite shocked to see its deplorable condition. From the street, the single-story concrete building looked barely occupiable. When I first got to Bali, Danny mentioned that the damage from the quake was much more widespread in the rural and suburban outskirts of the island. I was seeing firsthand the extent of that damage.

The school was located away from the city center and the cleanup crews didn't fully clear the area. I wrestled my way through the rusty gate as the hinges finally squealed to life and crossed the debris-littered courtyard to make my way to the front door of the building. It was ajar and also hanging precariously on its hinges. I gently nudged it open, fearing that too much force would cause it to topple over me.

The courtyard was nothing compared to the scene inside the building. It looked as if a tornado had been through the room. Better yet, it looked like the center of the earthquake was situated in this room. I gave myself a mental eyeroll and braced myself for what I was going to find beyond the first room.

I looked at my watch which read 8:30 a.m. I arrived a little bit earlier than the time Nugroho and I agreed upon. Not being one to stand around like a lump on a log, I decided to inspect the room to see the extent of the damages. I used my background in architecture and construction management to do a quick assessment of the concrete floors and walls, looking for obvious cracks and damages to the foundation. I saw none in the floor or what I perceived to be the load-baring walls.

Feeling a bit more confident about the stability of the structure, I took in the massive shell of a room that was strewn with broken desks, chairs, and tables. Glass from blown out windows glinted dangerously on the surfaces of the few tables and chairs that were still intact. Larger shards littered the floor near the windows.

"It looks like a fucking bomb went off in here," I muttered under my breath, now standing in the center of the main room and taking in the level of damage the space had taken. The brevity of the devastation in this room alone humbled me but strengthened my resolve to help out as much as I could.

Nugroho tried to warn me that there would be some cleanup required before we could start bringing in the students. He failed to mention just how much cleanup. I was moved to action but still had my inner doubts about making any impact on this mess before my time in Bali was up. Shit, I was only scheduled to be here just over a month and by the looks of the all cleanup that needed to be done, it would be time for me to go home before the first class convened.

In the far-left corner of the room, there was a broom and bucket that seemed to miraculously materialize out of the dust. Surprisingly, they seemed to be untouched by the earthquake. *Ok, God. Real funny.* I guess this was His way of telling my ass to *get to cleaning*. I grabbed the broom and bucket, emptying the dust and dirt that had settled in the bottom, and I propped both against the broken fence so as not to lose them.

I was relieved that I came dressed to clean because I was about to get dirty. I opted to wear thick white socks and Timberland boots. I knew it would be hot, so I wore cut-off jeans shorts and a black tank as my base. I threw on a long-sleeve red and black plaid lumberjack just in case there were yucky things that I didn't want to touch. Hot or not, I had on the long sleeves to make sure no creepy critters crawled on me. I shuddered at the thought.

I bought a cheap scarf while I was out with Danny the other day to wrap around my head. I was glad at the forethought because it would take five sets of hands to wash the dust out of my hair. After inspecting the room, I didn't see anything that would gross me out, so I opted to take the plaid work shirt off. I tied it around my waist and dove into the task of removing the large debris from the classroom.

An hour or so later, I stopped to take a break. I felt sweat running down my back and the crevice of my breasts. I jumped and shook my shirt thinking that something was crawling on me. I exhaled a sigh of relief and chuckled from the realization that it was just sweat running down my skin.

"Ahem."

I looked up in shock as I heard someone clear their throat over by the door. Across the room a slender, older man who must have been Nugroho stood in the doorway waving at me. He cleared his throat to get my attention, most likely not to scare me half to death. He walked over to me with his hand outstretched to shake mine. I quickly wiped my sweaty palm on the leg of my shorts and returned the gesture.

"Hello. You must be Rhiyan?" the gentleman asked.

"Yes, and you must be Nugroho?"

"I am. Please call me Gro," he said, giving me a kind, welcoming smile.

"Ok. Only if you call me Rhi," I smiled back, liking his gentle spirit.

"Deal."

"You have been working hard, I see," he said, clearly impressed as he walked further into the corner of the room where I had been working. He appraised the space, continuing to nod his head up and down as he turned back in my direction. The contrite look on his face mirrored his next words. "My apology, I *intents* to be *heres* before you *arrives* and *certunly* did *no'expects* for you to be cleaning *alones*."

"It's no problem," I said, noticing he added an 's' to his words in similar fashion as Danny, so I had no problem understanding him. "I got here early and decided to just get started while I waited."

"*Thanks yur*. This *amazing*," he said, hands now on his hips as he gave the room another look.

He continued assessing my work while simultaneously pulling off his grey jacket. Underneath, he wore an old, dingy T-shirt which indicated he was prepared for work as well. I inspected him further to see he had on a pair of khaki work pants and work boots too. He wasn't a big guy but was wiry and looked like he could carry some of the heavier debris from the room.

He started picking up trash and carrying it out the doorway. I jumped back in and continued cleaning the corner of the room that I had been working on all morning. We worked steadily and in silence for a while, both of us caught up in our own work.

Gro was carrying more trash out to the curb, breaking the silence as he entered the room, "I was *lates* because I was trying to round up the *o-thur* volunteers *thats* was to be here," he said as he stopped at the doorway, looking out at the street view. "*Buts* some of the roads still *outs*. Today, just you and me, but *tomorrows* a structural *engineers* be onsite to make sure building is safe."

"That is good to know," I said, propping my chin atop my hands that rested on top of the broom handle. "I walked around and checked for any structural damage when I first got here. I didn't see any, but it is good to know that the building will be fully checked out."

"*Safetys* is *er* top priority," he continued. "I think I read on *yours volunteers* application that you are *engineers* too?" His eyes were gleaming with curiosity.

"I work closely with the engineers at the architectural firm that I work for," I answered. "But I'm more so on the construction management and commercial development side of the house."

"*Impressives*. This building one of a *fews commercials* building in the area that still *standings*," he stated matter-of-factly. "It was erected after last *bigs* earthquake; more structurally *sounds* due to stronger materials. *Mains* reasons why YUM choose location for the school."

"Good to know," I said, also impressed at his historical knowledge of the building and at YUM's thoroughness in ensuring the children's safety.

We spent the rest of the morning clearing debris. By the time we broke for lunch, half of the space was cleared out. It was beginning to take shape, complete with a few classrooms, albeit open-air classrooms since the single-story building still had no windows.

Gro asked me what I had brought for lunch. I was washing my hands in a bucket of water and offhandedly responded, "I didn't bring anything. Figured I'd just grab some noodles from a street vendor."

"Umm, Rhi... I don't know if *yous* notice, but homes and buildings all *topples* up and down this street. No street vendor for miles."

I stood, wiping my hands on the shirt tied around my waist.

"Shit," I stammered. I clapped my hand to my forehead, slightly embarrassed at the oversight. I looked at him with a wry smile and lifted brows. "I guess I didn't think that through at all."

Standing beside Gro in the doorway facing the street, I noticed for the first time how devastated the rest of the area really was. The roof of the two-story concrete building next to us was caved in; the awning of the gas station across the street was ripped away; abandoned cars were parked in disarray. It was a sad sight to behold. It was dark when I arrived this morning, so I didn't notice any of this.

"*Stills* pretty *bads*," Gro said almost verbatim to Danny's comments my first day here, his features contorting into a sullen downcast expression.

He walked over and patted me on the back in genuine concern before saying, "In the *aftermaths* of the quake, there were *manys* missing and buried *peoples* under the rubbish. Yet, the *peoples* here are optimistic and *er recovers good*." This sudden flash of hope, despite its transient and ephemeral quality, was contagious. I found myself feeling a bit more positive and upbeat. The sadness that was weighing on my chest dissipated; even though my eyes dreadfully swept the expanse of the work that was waiting for us to complete. Gro helped me reencounter the 'why' of my being there. He reminded me of the heart-felt reason I decided to come to Bali in the first place.

"I was compelled to come here," I stated a bit nervously, "and it is why I think it is so important that we get the school and recreation center ready for these kids. I'm glad I can offer this little sliver of sunlight and help make this," I waved my outstretched hand around at the space in front of us, "a sanctuary for the children as the island is rebuilt."

"Come." Gro grabbed my hand excitedly. "Walk *withs* me. My home is *no* far, and my wife fix us lunch."

"Thank you," I said, pressing my fingers together in steepled prayer as I graciously accepted his offer. My stomach seemed to thank him too as it growled loudly in hunger. That was our signal to go.

As we walked the four or five blocks, Gro broke the silence as I took in more of the devastation. "We lucky enough to *haves er generators* to *keeps* the food. Now that the electricity is back, many of us get together for *er* how do you say," he paused to think through an English equivalent, "*potlucks* lunches and dinners with our families. Help keep everyone in a good *moods*."

I contemplated his words as I took in more of the devastation the earthquake had wreaked on this slice of paradise. However, the last block brought us to a neighborhood of small cinder block homes on a peaceful street lined with palm trees. It looked almost untouched by the quake aside from the ripples and small buckles in the pavement. This was Gro's neighborhood.

He explained that not many homes in his neighborhood had been damaged, but the gas lines under the streets were. The city cut the flow of gas and though they had water for bathing, it could not be heated or used for cooking. The emergency management agency provided water for drinking and cooking.

As we got closer to his home, I could hear faint music and smell the hint of cooked meats and spices in the air. My missed meal cramps grew stronger from the smell of barbecue. When Gro's home was finally in sight, the scene was almost a replica of my father's famous cookouts. The music was different, but it looked like a Bali BBQ was in full swing.

Gro introduced me to his neighbors while blocking a ball that was coming straight for my face, kicked by one of the many children playing in the yard. He turned to me smiling and then bent down to ruffle the hair of the cutest little six-year-old I had ever seen. She was missing two front teeth but looked up at me with big open eyes full of wonder. Her sweet little face and inquisitive eyes tugged at my core.

"Rhi, this my daughter. Naijah, introduce yourself."

She shyly slid from behind her father's legs where she was half hiding, half gawking at me and nervously reached out her hand for a shake.

"I'm Naijah," she said as the corners of her mouth curled up into a big and very toothless grin. "You look like Beyonce!" she blurted before retreating back behind her father's leg again.

That didn't surprise me, as just the other day, another local had asked if I were related to Barack Obama. Everybody knew Beyonce and Barack. Plus, the Beehive was international. I wasn't mad at the reference.

"Well, that is the sweetest thing anyone has ever told me," I said before covering my mouth to stifle my giggle. I kneeled down to the child's level and stuck my hand back out for another shake.

"I'm Rhi. It is a pleasure to meet you, Naijah... and you are more beautiful than Princess Jasmine from Aladdin." Her blank facial expression reflected her lack of knowledge on the classic fairytale. So, I added, "She is the most beautiful Disney princess of them all."

At that, she gave me another toothless grin before skipping off to continue playing kickball with her friends. I watched Gro watch

Naijah. He looked like the proudest papa on Earth. He looked at me and nodded. "I *thinks* you have captivated my little one, *Beyonces*."

We shared a laugh as he took me by the elbow and walked me over to meet his wife, Wayan. I later learned that the traditional naming system in Bali denoted birth order. Wayan meant first born. By that logic, I understood why I had met so many Ketuts since my arrival. It literally meant fourth born. And here I was thinking that Ketut, the character that Julia Roberts was translating for in the movie *Eat Pray Love* had such a unique name... *Not*.

The traditional Balinese lunch we had was delicious and the atmosphere was quite festive. I was glad for this because, the walk to Gro's neighborhood was quite depressing. We prepared ourselves to head back over to the school to finish up for the day. I thanked Wayan and said goodbye to my new friends. I was pleasantly surprised when Naijah ran over, gave me a hug, and asked if I would come back tomorrow to play with her. I ruffled the kiddo's hair and told her we'd have to see about that.

Chapter 9 - Rhiyan

NOT MUCH WORK WAS done after we finished up lunch with Gro's family. We walked back over to the work site basking under the warm afternoon sun, both of us in a more gleeful mood than before.

"Rhiyan, I am so pleased you onboard *withs* us… and it looks like you have made a new fan in Naijah."

"Oh stop," I said waving off the fan comment, "She is such a beautiful and funny child, Gro. You and Wayan have trouble on your hands. Better get the shotgun ready."

Gro laughed out loud at that, releasing a heavy sigh that said, 'Oh, I already know that…'

Gro pulled a couple of buckets to the center of the school courtyard and nodded for me to sit across from him. We spent the rest of the afternoon mapping out a plan to finish the cleanup and decided that we would try to open up doors next Monday. That would give us six days to have the place ready and set up for learning and recreation.

Just as we were wrapping up, Gro's cell rang. It was odd hearing that sound because I had no service since touching down in Bali. He mumbled "satellite phone" when he noticed the confused expression on my face.

I busied myself with putting the buckets away and closing up the center as best I could before we prepared to leave for the day. Bookbag on my back, I stood waiting for Gro to finish up his call. I could tell it was all business by the way he motioned his hands melodramatically as if he were giving instructions to the other person on the call. He hung up and walked over to me.

"Good news! We have four volunteer that will be joining us *tomorrows* to help with the cleanup."

"Awesome! We definitely will have the center ready in six days with the extra hands."

He nodded cheerfully and said, "Yes... and Rhi, I would *likes* you to take charge of the volunteers and *ensures* they know what they should be doing. I will be a bit late tomorrow since I have to *picks* them up and go to *talks* to the magistrate to get the proper licenses to clear us to open. Think you can handle?"

"Absolutely," I smiled in reassurance. "This place is going to be amazing in a few days."

"Oh, and the inspectors will be stopping by the *sites* tomorrow. It should only be *er* quick walk through to issue the official *buildings* certificate," he said shoving his hands in his pockets, sweeping his eyes around the courtyard and the building. "The building is fine. This is *alls* formality so we can officially *opens*."

If you say so, I thought knowing full well the red tape to get this building open in the states would have taken months to get through.

"While I'm *outs,* I will *gets* help to scavenge some of the other buildings to *finds* tables and chairs so we could have a learning area set up before the kids *arrives* next week."

"Yeah," I nodded. "That works. In the meantime, I will work with the volunteers to create an inviting layout for the space," my eyes brightened at the possibilities. "And we can work together to determine how best to set up the learning area..." I stopped to think then let the rest of the idea tumble out. "And perhaps a reading   roo-"

Incessant honking interrupted our conversation. My ride had arrived. Gro waved me off. "Go! Go! We *talks* further about *tomorrows.*"

"Ok, great," I said before entering the van. "See you then."

The short, 30-minute ride back to my resort was peaceful. The grueling work that Gro and I put in at the school had left me covered in grime from head-to-toe. My hair was dank and the mixture of sweat and dirt created a sticky glue-like film over my skin. I couldn't wait to get to my room to wash off the day.

In a hurry to do just that, I walked into the dimly lit open-air lobby, catching a glimpse of myself in one of the many floor-to-ceiling mirrors. I grimaced at my reflection and sped up even more to get to my room, rummaging through my bookbag to fish the key card to my room out as quickly as possible. As soon as I felt the cool stiffness of the plastic, I triumphantly spun left in a dash down the corridor to the bank of elevators that would take me to my floor. *Wham!* I ran smack dab into one of the hotel staff.

The thin porter flew one way, and I flew the other, the contents of my bookbag scattering across the floor. It took a moment to catch my bearings. I scrambled to my knees and tried to recover my belongings in the dim light while profusely apologizing to the young man I mowed down in my haste. He still had not recovered from his fall yet.

I quickly scooped up the loose contents that escaped during my tumble and secured them in my bag. I scanned its interior to ensure I had everything when a thick baritone voice, coming from above greeted my ears, "I think this belongs to you."

He held out my cellphone, which apparently flew much further across the lobby during my fall, in his palm.

That voice... It made the back of my neck tingle. It was deep. Masculine. Commanding almost. It unarmed me. There was no accent in this voice. *American?* Surprising because I hadn't run into any other Americans in all my time here.

I had a compulsion to see what the lips that belonged to the voice looked like. My desire to investigate started with his shoes. Dark brown, polished leather. *Cole Haan.* My curiosity was peaked even further because he wasn't wearing flip flops like everyone else lounging at the bar or on the comfortable chairs scattered about the lobby. Roaming further up, I took in the dark blue slacks. Muscular calves and thighs bulged through the fine fabric. I saw my phone in his outstretched hand again but ignored it and the cracked screen to study the massive, tanned fingers that were gripping it. They were strong fingers with clean, cotton candy-pink nail beds. I sat there staring at his hand like an idiot.

"Ma'am," he said in an impatient voice, snapping me out of the trance I was in. "Your phone..."

Maybe it was because I was tired or perhaps because I was embarrassed as hell from falling on my ass in front of all these other guests in the lobby, but that impatient tone of his voice pissed me off and made my back stiffen.

My eyes snapped to his, or where his eyes would have been had they not been covered by dark aviator sunglasses. Oh, the trance was definitely gone now, replaced with a hot desire to snatch the offensive mirror-tinted lenses off his face and break them.

A single brow raised arrogantly from behind the stupid sunglasses as he shook the phone in my face again. This arrogant motherfucker had the nerve to stare down at me like he wanted to say, 'Get this damn phone, so I can get back to my drink.'

Without a word, I snatched my phone and secured it in my bag. Then I stood fully erect, slung the bag that had gotten me into this mess over my shoulder, and prepared to walk away. Thinking back to my home training, though, I took a deep breath to calm myself and decided to thank this rude man and keep it moving. *Big mistake.* I got sidetracked by his chiseled jawline and slightly full lips atop what had to be at least 6 foot 3 inches of sinewy muscle. Then he opened his stupid mouth again, saying the rudest shit I heard in a long time.

"You should be more careful and look where you are going."

Oh fuck no. Who did this ogre think he was talking to? At this point, he pushed the wrong buttons. I decided in that moment I would not dignify his smart-ass comment with a response. I mumbled a very decisive 'fuck you' and turned on my heel, giving him my whole ass to kiss as I made a beeline for my room.

Who the hell wears sunglasses at night? I thought as I began stripping the dirty clothes away from my tired and aching body, leaving them in a heap at the foot of the bed. All I cared about at this moment was a long, cold shower. A *very* cold shower. Irritation personified as I realized how that voice had done something to me. Those *shades* had done exactly the opposite.

The icy cold water felt like needles piercing my skin. It would eventually get warm, but right now, I needed it to cool my hot ass off.

The fuck! Who wears sunglasses at night? I thought again as I roughly scrubbed at my skin like I was trying to rip it off along with the dirt. I knew exactly who wears sunglasses at night. Kyle. Shoulders slumping, I lowered my head letting out a pained sigh. My cheeks and neck burned as my shoulders slumped in shame under the pelting spray of the water. I literally just showed my ass in that lobby because a stranger's ridiculous notion to wear sunglasses at night reminded me of my ex.

But it was more than that. Yes. The sunglasses were the trigger, but his impatience was all too familiar; making me feel... *inadequate.* Also, a left-over emotion from my marriage to a man who made it his business to try to tear me down. If it wasn't my hair, it was my weight and when none of those worked, he attacked my success trying to minimize my professional accomplishments by making me feel as though I couldn't be a good wife and successful at work at the same time. All of that on top of not being able to make a Kyle Junior.

I'd tried to hold on to a marriage that was destined to fail; making me feel all the more stupid and all the more triggered by any reminder of it.

Not willing to let it go, my pride had me teetering between holding on to my irritation and the shame. I decided to stay pissed. Not at the lobby guy, *sort of*. I was pissed at myself and the fact that I was still allowing Kyle's ol' cheating ass to affect me in such a way.

Nah. Fuck that. I bet Mr. Nice Shoes was an arrogant prick, too. It was apparent by the smirk he wore as he looked down at me. Probably thought I was some backpacking, dirty American looking to rob somebody. I didn't feel so bad for being rude once I remembered his impatient ass look and that rude comment about watching where I was going. *Who the hell was he supposed to be?*

And now, I was teetering again. *Was he being rude?* I questioned myself in doubt. Being a little gentler to my skin now, I allowed the scene in the lobby to replay again in my head. His voice was undeniably sexy. It was clear, yet very low-pitched and full. It was perplexing because he definitely had the timbre of a brother, but his skin tone gave nothing away about his identity. It was the color of sun-kissed sand, perfectly smooth in the softly lit room. His hair texture provided no clues because from my not-so-great vantage point on the floor, he appeared to be totally bald.

That voice though... it stirred my soul a little bit. I lost any interest in dating since the divorce and honestly didn't even have a desire to have my yoni stroked. *Not until now!* I felt my unruly lady parts respond. Amazing how he pissed me off and turned me on at the same time. *Ugh*, I groaned.

I didn't realize I had begun rubbing the warm soapy washcloth over my lady parts until a moan escaped my lips. *Damn...* that voice. That voice had me slowly spreading my legs as wide as I could in the narrow shower and detaching the shower head to focus the firm spray directly on my pearl. I rested my forehead against the cool shower wall as waves of pleasure radiated from my core as I came violently against the nozzle.

I slowly came down from my shower induced fireworks. Satisfied, yet still perplexed and slightly embarrassed that his voice did that to me. *Shit. What is wrong with me?* A complete stranger almost unleashes my ratchet and rude self and the very same stranger has me masturbating in the shower like a horny teenager.

Chapter 10 —Kendrick

I SAW HER WHEN she walked into the lobby; a stark contrast to the other patrons milling about. They all wore chic resort wear. *She* looked like she had been doing construction work. But even covered in dirt from her wild, reddish-gold mane to her nubuck Timberland clad feet, she was stunning. Her hair was in a messy bun, high atop her head with a few whisps of hair tumbling over her brow stuck to her dirt-streaked forehead. The style accentuated a long, elegant neck while the damp v-neck t-shirt did the same for her full breasts and slim waist. *Was I dreaming?*

It was my first time at this resort and had arrived only an hour before, but I had visited Bali and other places in Indonesia many times before. I had never seen a sistah as fine as this one on any of those previous trips. Hell, I wasn't sure if I had ever seen a sexier woman. *Period.* Not in Bali for damn sure. Knowing I probably looked crazy as hell this time of night, I was glad for the shades covering what I knew to be blood-shot eyes from the lack of sleep on that long-ass flight. Anyone paying half attention could see the lust in my eyes for this woman from a mile away.

Her cut off, denim shorts, *got damn*. Those shorts molded to the swell of her wide hips and thick, copper thighs. This must be what they meant by *Black Girl Magic* because baby girl had me mesmerized. I was fighting the thought of those long, shapely legs wrapped around my waist when, *wham!*

My mini fantasy was cut short as I watched her tumble to the floor. Shit flew everywhere. The Jameson I was sipping on and the thoughts of her legs must have slowed my reaction time, or else I would have been able to yell out just in time to warn her. Instead, I watched the scene unfold before me in slow motion. *Damn.* She fell hard.

She was walking head down rifling through her bag when the porter came around the corner and they collided. Even though I had on shades in the dim light of the lobby, I still managed to see her cell phone go airborne. I visibly winced as it bounced, clattered, and slid across the polished stone floor of the lobby, stopping just in front of my seat.

I put my drink down in a hurry and picked the phone up, noticing the cracked glass screen, pushing up out of my seat without hesitation to walk the short distance to return it to her. *What did I do to deserve this luck?*

I walked over preparing to hit her with a panty-dropper smile and held out her phone. *She was even more lovely up close.* I stood directly over her, waiting for our eyes to meet. When she looked up, her eyes were far from smiling which led me to freeze. She stared at me as if she had seen a ghost, and the color drained right out of her face. Regaining some of her composure, the shock on her face gave way to pure disdain. Her lips pursed like she was about to snarl. Then she abruptly snatched the phone out of my hand.

Perplexed, I almost snatched my shades off to get a better look at this feisty angel but didn't get a chance. *Did I know her? Had I smashed and left her hanging?* Nah. I would have remembered this firecracker. So why was she so hostile towards me?

I didn't know what to say to her at this point. A little thrown off, all I could think to say was, "You should be more careful and aware of your surroundings." I'm sure my tone was wrong, but I was reacting to the attitude she was shooting my way.

With that, she stood abruptly, and shot me a quick, "Fuck you," before turning tail. She was halfway around the corner, leaving me standing there, mouth wide open, looking dumb as hell.

I walked back over to my seat but didn't sit. I picked up the glass and tossed the rest of the Jameson back, allowing the hot liquid to singe the back of my throat before slamming the glass on the table and going to my room. My previous relaxed mood was a bit fucked up as I entered my room brooding.

I decided I wasn't going to give that long-legged vixen another thought. I had work to do before my meeting with the Minister of Interior the next day and used it as a welcome distraction from my thoughts of the Devil's spawn from the lobby.

I needed to walk the minister and his staff through the reconstruction plans that we put together for the recovery of the island and surrounding areas. Since sleep was not going to be my friend tonight, I rehearsed the presentation I had prepared. About 10 minutes in, I realized that I was reading the same slide over and over. I couldn't shake the images of fiery wild hair, reddish-caramel skin, high cheekbones, and slanted eyes.

I wondered what she was doing here. Bali, especially this resort in Nusa Dua, was a notoriously swanky vacation spot. Why was she here looking like she was working on a construction site? In my line of business, I dealt with lots of weathered and tough-skinned laborers, tradesmen, and women, but absolutely zero with the divine femininity of the hellion I had the pleasure and displeasure of meeting earlier.

I gave up on getting any work done. I knew I was already prepared, so I wasn't concerned. I showered quickly and decided to lay it down for the night. Before my eyes closed and my head hit the pillow, I fantasized burying my face in that beautiful mane of hers. Exasperated, I flipped on my stomach and slammed the cold pillow over my head trying to block the image and coax my stiff dick into behaving. Too late. Morning couldn't come quick enough.

The receptionist escorted me through the glass doors of the Minister of the Interior's office. I was a familiar face in the building and I knew my way around well enough. I walked in and was greeted by Ketut Bhangan, the minister. He was like family to me, so we skipped the formal introductions and grasped hands before pulling each other into a full embrace. He patted my back like a father greeting his son.

"Everyone, you remember Kendrick."

Several of the heads swiveled towards the two of us in greeting as Ketut warmly said, "It has been too long my friend. We missed you last Christmas."

"I know," I replied, taking a seat in one of the empty chairs near Ketut's. "I couldn't get away on holiday. Workloads tripled after the big volcano eruption last summer. You know how it is. A natural disaster strikes and Kekoa is there."

"Unfortunately, business must be booming for you as a result of the unnaturally high number of natural disasters that are hitting every country in the world. Hence, the reason we are all here today."

With that, the meeting was underway. I caught the fleeting glimpse of sadness in his eyes before the mask of a broad smile plastered on his face. He expertly made his opening remarks and shared his goals for the reconstruction of his beloved Bali. Before turning the meeting over to me, he gave me a deep sobering look then continued, "You have had your fair share of disasters, Kendrick. I'm just glad that we can depend on you and Kekoa Industries to help us and the neighboring islands recover."

"That's what I am here for," I assured him and laid out the plans for the reconstruction effort.

I founded Kekoa Industries 17 years ago after working as a civil engineer on projects all around the world. We are the largest architectural and civil engineering firm in the Hawaiian Islands; specializing in natural disaster cleanup, assessment, and reconstruction, called on to consult federal, civil, and municipal governments across the world.

Freakish weather systems of late kept us pretty busy. We were no strangers to this area of the world, often known as the Ring of Fire for its many active volcanoes. These hot beds were the culprit for many earthquakes and tsunamis that were frequent in the Lombok and Bali regions of Indonesia. Yet, this place had a hold on my heart ever since I was a *keiki*, a small child, nipping at my mother's heels when she brought me along with her those many years ago on a mission for Doctors Without Borders. That's how I first met Ketut and his family. I'd been back several times over the years after my mother's death. They were like family, and Bali was like a second home to me.

We sat down and I ran through the comprehensive reconstruction plan with Ketut and his people. "I want to stress how important it is that me and my crew get on the ground as soon as possible to begin the building and life safety assessments. That's priority number one to ensure we minimize any more casualties and the number of buildings at risk of caving in."

There was no telling what we were going to find after we started the cleanup and debris removal, but I wanted it to be my guys to find anything unsettling rather than a family member out searching for a loved one. Ketut and his staff seemed to read between the lines, and all unanimously agreed with the proposed plan. Ketut signed off without question and promised to provide the full resources of the government to ensure we could get the island back up and running without unnecessary red tape.

The plan was to start the assessments at the hospitals and then radiate out in concentric sweeps to ensure every building was evaluated and certified as inhabitable. My smaller tiger teams would start at the government service buildings, schools, and public work sites to get water, gas, and electricity grids back up and kids back in school. Restoring normalcy was the goal; secondary to that was to rebuild as quickly as possible using our state-of-the-art sustainable products and methods to help reinforce some of the buildings and roads to withstand the next earthquake or tsunami that would inevitably come.

Before I left the Minister's office, Ketut grabbed me in a tight embrace again and stood back to look me over.

"Kendrick, I am so proud of the man you have become. We love you here like you are a native to the island." He paused briefly to compose himself. The sadness from earlier, now on full display in his tear-glazed eyes. "After your mother died, I promised myself that I would check on you and provide whatever support I could. I know it wasn't much with you being back home with your dad and family in Hawaii but know that you have always been in Ria's thoughts and mine... in our hearts as well. We are so proud of you, son." He quickly wiped the tear that escaped onto his cheek.

I patted him on the shoulder and walked out of the conference room before the tears I barely held at bay dropped.

I knew his sadness was more about the loss of my mother all those years ago. He didn't know I knew, but he was in love with her back then, and it was evident that he still missed her now. I could tell the pain of her loss still weighed heavy on his heart. I was a reminder of the love he lost, and he was a reminder for me, too. It took me a long time to forgive him because my mother was still married to my father when their affair began. I found out the truth years later, and I came to terms with it. I was able to forgive them both wholeheartedly without holding a grudge.

I began to come back here every year on the anniversary of my mother's death and over the years built a pretty close relationship with Ketut and his family, his wife Ria, and their four sons Gede, Kadek, Komang, and Ketut. They treated me like another member of the family; I too felt like I was a part of theirs. I never told my biological father about the affair. He had been through enough with losing his wife and having to raise a son as a single parent back in Hawaii.

I decided to walk back to my hotel from the meeting rather than grabbing a hired car. I wanted to smell the ocean and get lost in the sounds of the bustling city center of the island.

There were visible signs of the destruction from the quake on almost every building. Cracks in foundations, broken windows, boarded up openings. But looking at the people who were carrying on about their business, you couldn't tell that less than a week ago, their lives were literally rocked by the 7.0 quake.

Chapter 11 – Rhiyan

I WALKED THROUGH THE wooden doors of the center. The first thing I noticed was that the door didn't squeak. It was actually on its hinges. Then, I noticed the easy banter of several unfamiliar voices beyond the main room. Intermixed in the sound of voices was a cacophony of sound. Hammers hitting nails, the whirring sounds of drills, tables, and chairs scraping against concrete floors. All welcomed noises that signaled work was in progress.

I found the source of the voices and laughter. Gro was engrossed in an animated conversation with a small group of four new faces, the other volunteers I assumed. I caught his attention as I made my way into the room.

"Rhi, come on *overs*," he waved, encouraging me to close the distance between myself and the small group.

"You're here, already!" I said a bit surprised. "I thought you were going to be late today?"

"The volunteers were *readys* for me to *picks* them up earlier than I *thoughts*, so we *cames* straight *aways*," he beamed around the room. "Look at *alls* that they have accomplished!"

"Wow!" I said, eyes following the same path as his. "This is amazing!" I said, making eye contact with each of them and back to Gro, expectantly waiting for him to make introductions.

"They just got *heres* two hours ago and their *youths* has already put me to shame!" he said, sounding like a happy uncle. "*Everyones*, this is Rhiyan, who I told you about *earliers*. Rhi here is from the United States; Atlanta, to be *exacts*," he stated with flourish before proceeding to rattle off each name of the new volunteers in introduction.

I picked up several different accents as they all said 'hello' and shook my hand. Perhaps mostly European. Definitely a French accent. It belonged to Dominic, a flamboyant, handsome young man with wavy, dark hair, a small wiry frame, and a hint of the devil in his eyes. I could tell he was the life of the party in the group.

The next accent was thick with a rich, sultry Latin flair. It belonged to Francis. She was Brazilian and the reserved one in the rag tag crew. Her raven-colored hair was pulled back into a sharp bun at the nape of her neck, toning down her understated beauty. I reached out and continued shaking hands as Gro continued the intros.

The next voice was unmistakably American. Unmistakably Texan. It belonged to Jeff, a gangly country boy with the tall lean body of a surfer. His unruly blonde hair was damn-near white at the tips. I knew why he was on this volunteer mission to Bali. *Surfing.* And last, but certainly not least, the last accent belonged to Jen, a Swedish bombshell, with Khalisi white, long blonde hair and an award worthy tan. She was stunning with long slender legs for days. Her height rivaled my own as she appeared to stand about an inch taller. She was the cool kid of the group. I could tell by the *'sup* nod she threw up at me as she reached to shake my hand with a warm smile.

"By the *ways*, Rhi got *heres* a little ahead of your group," Gro said waving a hand in a circle around at everyone. "She is responsible for *gettings* this place cleaned out and in the best *conditions*," he doted while looking at me.

"That was small in comparison to what you all have already accomplished. In what? Two hours?" I said, looking down at my watch at the still early hour. "And y'all have already moved in the furniture, finished the floors, and hung the cabinets and doors!"

Dominic, who didn't have on a shirt, flexed his pecks and held up a bicep, kissing it in gest before blowing me a jazz-fingered kiss. I knew he was a clown. I laughed at his antics while excitedly acknowledging everyone and their contributions with raised eyebrows of excitement. I clasped my hands together eagerly, doing a semi-circle back to Gro.

"We'll definitely be ready to open the doors to the children by the beginning of next week," I said, grinning from ear-to-ear.

At that, work commenced, and we all set out to get the school ready for opening day. I worked with Jeff and Dominic to put in the remaining windows. Grateful for their brawn and know-how because I was totally in the way. They carried the heavy panes and installed them like pros. *Little* Dominic was flirting hard with me and I was eating that shit up knowing full well he was probably more interested in the harder body variety. Whatever the case; gay, straight, or fluid - his flirting secretly flattered the cougar in me.

I turned away from the group to wipe the sweat away from my eyes with the corner of my shirt, being careful not to flash the young stallions with a peek-a-boo of my breasts. I squeezed them shut to soothe the last vestiges of burning. I blinked a few times then looked up only to come face-to-face with a furrowed brow and piercing eyes staring way too hard at my now covered chest.

"What the fuck!" I yelled as I recoiled and shrank back in shock.

"Who is in charge here?" A large booming voice emerged out of those disgruntled lips. "Nobody should be in this building!"

I held up my hand ready to snap, cutting his ass right back off.

"Hold up. *Who* the fuck you think you talking to like that?"

He continued on like I hadn't said a word, "I need you all to leave this building immediately by order of the Minister of Interior." He paused long enough to point those mirror-tinted aviators down at me.

Again. I scowled and blew out a hard sigh.

Not seeing the warning signs of my near eruption, his lip curled up slightly in a jeering smirk as he continued in a barely audible hiss directed at me, "This building has not been cleared yet and you all are trespassing."

Oh, he was fucking asking for it, but I held back, not wanting to show my ass for the second time on this arrogant bastard. My eyes flashed with fury. Instead of speaking, I stared him down, daring him to speak to me in such a tone again. He must have gotten the message because he pulled a card out of his pocket and shoved it towards me. I ignored the gesture.

"This shit again," he grumbled just loud enough for me to hear him.

I pursed my lips and folded my arms, holding my ground. I let the hand holding the card linger mid-air a beat longer as I trained my unblinking, deadpan stare directly at his face.

He sighed deeply like I was on his last nerve and stated in a stiff, measured tone, "My name is Kendrick Kekoa. I am in charge of the building safety assessment. I need you and your folks to clear out..."

He stared right back at me with the same dead-pan expression, daring me to defy the order.

Just as I was about to go straight up ham on his ass, we were both interrupted by Gro entering the room. We turned in unison in the direction of his voice.

"Gentleman, please. How may I help you?" he asked, head swiveling back and forth between me and the lead intruder, now revealed as Kendrick Kekoa. "I am Gro, and I've been given verbal clearance from the minister himself to begin getting this building ready for the children who will be occupying this space early next week. Please see the permits that I have," Gro said while rifling through his bag to pull out the signed papers from the minister.

Kendrick grabbed the papers without so much as glancing at them and handed them to the guy on his right. I was so hyper focused on this jerk that I didn't notice he had an entourage with him. His companion seemed as equally menacing—bulky, too, but not as tall—head adorned with a man-bun and arms covered in tribal tattoos. Without speaking, he handed the papers back to Gro and nodded at Kendrick. All the while, his apparent boss stood impossibly close to me—not once breaking the stare down.

In a calmer voice but still laced with venom, he said, "I understand that you have the right paperwork. But I wasn't aware of any buildings in this area being approved for use," he broke eye contact and pinned his gaze on Gro. "Please take your folks outside so my crew and I can do a quick assessment to ensure this building is safe. It will only take a few minutes, Miss...?" He brought his eyes back to mine in question.

"Rhiyan," I sucked my teeth and reaffirmed my stance, still glaring at him through squinted eyes.

"Ms. Rhiyan," he said, moving his hand up to cup his chin in an attempt to either lock it into memory or ponder its true meaning. "Thank you," he finally said, his muted anger translating into dark amusement.

"Out. *Now,*" he thumbed towards the door. As my jaw dropped in disbelief, he quickly rectified himself, "I'd hate for a sharp object to fall and hit you upside that pretty head of yours."

A few of the men in his group chuckled as they walked past me to start the inspection.

I rolled my eyes and before I could give this insolent bastard a piece of my mind, Gro grabbed my elbow and led me to the door while signaling for the other volunteers to join us outside as well. He gave me a bewildered, but reassuring look before saying loud enough for everyone to hear, "Yes, let's let these fine men assess the building. I'm sure all will be in order, and we can get back to it shortly."

"Gentlemen," Gro nodded back at Kendrick and his crew as we walked through the front door into the courtyard to wait.

Outside, I paced back and forth, swearing under my breath at his arrogance. I must have had a deep scowl on my face since Gro cautiously asked me, "Are you okay?"

His question startled me; I looked up at him like I just noticed his presence. He cleared his throat and said, "That exchange between you two was pretty..." he paused to seek the right word, "intense. Do you know him?"

I looked away briefly as a memory of our exchange last night pervaded the chambers of my mind. I answered truthfully, "No. I don't know *Mr. Rude*. He just came in making demands as if he owned the place."

"Could have fooled me, Ms. Rhi," I heard Dominic say from a few feet away, making the whole gang burst out laughing.

He gave me a conspiratorial wink before adding, "That was a lot of big dick energy he was giving off back there," Dominic chuckled, directing his gaze past the doorway at the muscle-headed jerk. He sauntered off to rejoin the other volunteers, singing softly in his thick French accent, *"There must be something there that wasn't there before..."*

I rolled my eyes.

The other members of the group gave me slick looks as if to agree with Dominic that there was something between Kendrick "fucking" Kekoa and I. I gave all of them a scorching look that clearly should have halted all of those silly thoughts. But it didn't.

One of the female volunteers looked at me coyly and winked. "I'll climb that tall, thick tree if you're not interested," she teased. The small group laughed hysterically as I hushed them repetitively in vain.

Ten minutes later, the brute and his henchmen exited the school. Kendrick walked over to where Gro and I were standing. He addressed his words to Gro and yet, fixated his gaze on me. *Is he trying to intimidate me?* I thought sarcastically. I held the glare.

"The building is safe for you all to enter," he said, giving his full attention to Gro now. "My crew will be back later this week to do a more thorough inspection. I do not believe we will find anything wrong, but we need to out of abundant caution for your safety." He paused briefly to look down his nose at me. "And anyone else's safety."

I couldn't help but feel an unspoken challenge arising between us, and my aura screamed '*Game on!*' His pursed lips and lifted eyebrows responded in affirmation before he walked towards the work van that his team had entered minutes ago. Over his shoulder, he gave a dismissive and curt, "Ms. Rhiyan," then they were gone.

The group of volunteers, again erupted in laughter as I stood there looking like I had sucked a lemon.

"Oh, get back to work!"

Even Gro was chuckling as he walked past me to go back into the school.

Chapter 12 - Kendrick

T HEY DIDN'T EVEN WAIT for the door to close completely in the van before the crew went in on me. It started with Micah. "So, *uh*, you get those digits?" he asked.

Another team member said from the back of the van, "Red, wanted to fuck you up for staring at her titties!"

Another stated, "Man did you see the rack on her?"

I had to damn near yell over the guffaws and laughter to tell them to cool it. Not only was I uncomfortable with them cracking jokes at my expense, but I also felt the urge to defend Vixen from all this toxic masculinity. "Man, shut your ass up! You're talking about a lady," I yelled over the ruckus.

"Oh, *yeah*, she's a lady," Micah shot over at me from the driver's seat. "A lady man-eater, *braddah!* You might have met your match with that one."

I chuckled and shook my head before adding, "Let's go get these hungry fools lunch before I have to fire everybody and assemble myself a better crew."

They all yelled in unison, "Good luck! We're brahs for life, brah!"

"Brahs for life," I repeated, shaking my head but taking the jokes on the chin. "Micah, after lunch drop me off back at the resort. I need to call Jada before it gets too late."

I made it back to my room around 2 p.m. Bali time, making it 8 p.m. back home. Perfect timing as Jada and Ona were most likely finishing up dinner.

The phone rang almost five times before someone answered, I was just about to hang up when I heard her voice.

"Hello."

I knew instantly who the voice belonged to, and anger surged up my spine like a reverse trail of hot lava.

"Jade, what the fuck are you doing there?"

"Kendrick," she said in a dry tone. "I'm here spending time with my daughter. What else would I be doing here?"

"Oh, you mean the daughter who you forgot to pick up from school last month when she had to stay behind for tutoring? Or maybe the daughter who was looking for her mother at her gymnastics meet a couple of weeks back?" I was intentionally being the jackass she always portrayed me to be. "Nah, perhaps the daughter who hasn't seen or heard from you in over two weeks while you were out getting high out of your damn mind. That daughter?"

"Fuck you, Kendrick! You're always in my shit. That's why I never come around anymore!"

"Nah, fuck that. We both know why you don't come around and it has nothing to do with me being in your shit. As a matter of fact, where is Ona?"

"Her and Jada are out back," she said a little less ratchet this time. "We're chilling. Ona cooked and said it was all right for me to stay a few days. Stop tripping. Me and Jada been catching up... and I know I fucked up. I'm going to make it up to her. I just want to spend some time with my baby girl. Is that all right with you?"

Everything in me wanted to tell her ass to kick rocks and stay the fuck away from Jada, but I knew I couldn't. Jade was at the very least, her biological mother, but Ona was the closest thing Jada ever had to a mom or grandmother. If Ona felt that Jade was in her right mind and wouldn't traumatize Jada with her meth-antics, I wasn't going to make her leave. But I'd be damned if I was going to continue talking to her. "Put Jada on the phone," I said as controlled as I possibly could without popping a blood vessel in my strained neck.

"Hey, Pops!" Jada said in her happy go-lucky voice.

"Hey, Popcicle! What's popping?" My voice regained its normal pitch. I was relieved not to find a strain of stress in my baby girl's voice. Recently, Jada started getting really introverted when her mother was in the wind or when she broke one of the many promises she made to our baby girl to pick her up from school or hang out with her as typical moms do. Today, she seemed like her normal self. I didn't press on it because I didn't want to upset her.

"How's school going?" I asked.

"School is 100," she said in her tween slang. "You know they be tryin' a sistah and all, but I'm the smartest kid in the building."

"Fo' sho'," I said, amping my baby girl up.

"School is handled, son," she said before bursting into a fit of laughter. I couldn't help but laugh at our silliness, too.

"I see somebody's been in my 90's DVD collection again."

"Yeah, son," she said again, staying in character a little while longer.

"Yeah, I got your son! How is school, clown?" I yelled in my best *New Jersey Drive*-inspired accent, joining her again. We both laughed out loud at that before Jada straightened up and gave me the answer I was waiting for. "Dad, you know school is good. Remember that project you helped me with before my last gymnastics meet?"

"How could I forget? You had me up until 3 a.m. doing your project while you laid on the couch snoring."

"Egggg...zageration!" she said as if hacking out a sneeze, "I got an A on it!" she continued excitedly.

"That's good stuff. Proud of myself for getting you an A."

"Oh, come on!" she yelled. I could almost see her eyes growing big with her bottom lip falling, mouth wide in shock. "You didn't even do that much."

"Jada, you come on! If I didn't use these big strong hands of mine to hold all that scrap metal and wood together, you would have F.A.I.L.E.D!" I spelled the letters out to get under her skin even more.

"Whatever, Pops. You did help hold it down but only so I could glue the pieces of the rollercoaster model together. It was my design and my hard work that made the marble stay in motion for the required 10 seconds of the experiment!"

"Is that right?" I asked, clutching my chest incredulously, pausing just long enough to make her think I thought her logic was flawed.

"You know I'm right, Dad! Even though you really didn't help, I appreciate what little you did to get me that A!"

"*Tuh*... well, thanks for the thanks."

"You know what?" she asked, pausing for effect, "I should just go to college to be a scientist since I OWNED THAT CENTRIPETAL FORCE PROJECT!" she yelled like there was a crowd going wild somewhere. The crowd was me. I was the crowd that amped her up, clapping, going wild with the crowd noises and all for my baby girl.

"Congratulations! You did that, Jada!" A little less pumped, I continued, "Other than school, how's everything else going?" I was hoping she'd give some clue as to how she really felt about her mother popping up out of the blue. And judging by her answer, she knew me like the back of her hand.

"All good in the neighborhood, Dad. Oh, and don't worry. If she leaves tomorrow and we don't hear from her in the next month, at least I got to lay eyes on her. I'm fine. I know you and TiTi don't get along with her, but I'm glad TiTi let her stay."

I didn't want to ask but my 12, almost 13-year-old, was the smartest, funniest, most intuitive person I knew.

"Ok, Popcicle," was all I could say before telling her I loved her. "Put your TiTi on the phone."

"Love you too, Pops," she said before yelling like a banshee to call Ona to the phone. I could hear Ona coming in from the backyard yelling at Jada to stop yelling like she was crazy. Before relinquishing the phone to her TiTi, Jada whispered into the phone, "Dad, everything is good. You should stop being so hard on Mom. You know she got issues."

"Girl, give me that phone," I heard Ona say to Jada before she plucked the receiver from her hands.

"*Wen* are you coming *fo* get this little hellion out of my house?" she said through the receiver, feigning irritation at my Jada but doing a horrible job of it.

"Old lady, is that how you greet your favorite nephew?!"

"Favorite?" she cackled loudly slapping her thigh. "More like *only* nephew." Ona and I both laughed a little at that running joke we had every time I had to fly out with my team on an assignment. "Jada is doing fine, Kendrick. That mother of hers seems to be clean for now. So, I let her stay for Jada's sake."

Chapter 13 - Rhiyan

IT TOOK LESS THAN three days with the new volunteers on site to finish the cleanup, the painting, and all window installations at the school. We also managed to fix all the broken doors and hang fresh curtains that were donated by some of the local women from Gro's neighborhood; they were bright and sunny and gave the school a lively atmosphere that I knew the kids would love. By the time we arranged the tables and chairs in the designated learning areas, the place was ready. Monday was right around the corner, and we'd be opening the doors to the community kids bright and early at 9:00 on the dot.

It was nice working with the other volunteers. I was older than them, but we got along quite well. Spending time with Dominic, Francis, Jeff, and Jen was making me feel much better about my decision to come here. Dominic kept all of us in stitches. Jeff was the kindest country boy ever, and I could tell Francis was a bit smitten with him. Jen was a hoot. One would think her svelte beauty would have her haute nose in the sky, but she was actually the most down-to-earth of them all. It was so refreshing to see how free and spirited they all were.

Three days passed since that brute came in and basically kicked us out of the building. I honestly didn't know why I couldn't get him out of my head. *"Bitch, yes you do..."* I heard Jai's voice mocking me from across the world. I really could not stand him. I also struggled to understand why, which made him a problem. The real problem was that he made my uterus tickle unexplainably. We were oil and water, and that shit would not— could not mix. Yet, he was taking up way too much real estate in my mind.

It was still baffling to me why I disliked a man I knew nothing about so fervently. Yet, my tricky mind was see-sawing so much that I was getting all mixed up on the inside. One minute, I was wishing I could push him into a pool of hot lava and the very next minute, I was the pool of hot lava, yearning to lick his tattooed forearm. *Ugh. I had to admit, the man was Sexy with a capital S. The kind of fine Jai would call 'lose ya mind' fine.*

I thanked God that the impromptu visit to the building by him and his crew was not repeated because the horny schoolgirl in me would have ruined my cool determination to be unbothered. Micah, the foreman did come back to finish the assessment as promised. I couldn't miss the sly look on Micah's face when he said upon leaving, "Ms. Rhi, Kendrick sends his regards."

Kendrick sends his regards... Fuck Kendrick. I gave him a sarcastic smirk before rolling my eyes at his mischievous laughter as he and the skeleton crew exited the building. I was just glad that they completed their assessment and gave us the green light to open the school to the kids the next week. We worked hard to get this place ready, and it would have been a shame for us to have to delay the opening.

Since we finished everything early and wouldn't need to be on site for the weekend, we all decided to take advantage of the downtime before the center opened. It was Saturday and all of us were amped and ready to cut loose and explore the flavors of Bali.

The guys had plans to enjoy the waves down in Seminyak; I agreed to meet up with Francis and Jen to grab lunch in the nearby city center of Kuta. We planned to go to see a Balinese show that Jen heard promising things about from the concierge at the resort. Danny agreed to be our driver and ensured that he would get us to our destination and back.

The first stop was lunch at one of the swanky resorts along the way to Kuta. Then, we went to watch the sunset *Kekac* fire dance just outside one of the temples. The dancers' costumes were beautifully intricate; the acrobatics and dances told an amazing tale of a love that prevailed distance and loss. In the crowd, I saw the same chocolate sister who passed the eatery the other day. This time she was with a handsome guy. He was equally as chocolate and beautiful as her. Shit he was *fine*.

The young, brown-skinned lady looked to be about my age. When I caught her gaze, there was the same glimmer of excitement in her eyes as in our last encounter. The crowd was too thick for us to stop and chat, but we acknowledged each other with a friendly nod. A nod that said: *'I see you, sistah! You're not here alone.'*

While busy observing the other black girl, I lost Francis and Jen in the crowd as everyone left the show. It appeared that the crowd was moving down to the beach for a spontaneous concert that the drummers from the show were setting up. I stood peering through the crowd in search of the other ladies until I heard the festive music picking up on the beach below. I figured that was where they went, so I followed.

The atmosphere on the beach was more of a party vibe than the cultural one we just left. The drummers were playing a Caribbean flavored beat that got the crowd of mostly tourists in full-on party mode. Danny said the party never stopped in Bali. Earthquake be damned, he was right. The sultry music and heavy baselines had me feeling festive, too. Before long, I was joining the vibe of the other partiers and started swaying to the beat. That's when I spotted Jen. I waved until she spotted me and made her way over.

"Where's Francis?" I yelled over the loud music and rowdy dancers.

"She decided to go back to the resort. Said she wasn't feeling too well. Looks like we found the party."

I nodded in agreement. Shortly after, we were both lost in the music that seemed to be getting sultrier by the minute.

Jen began riding the beat, joining me in our own rendition of a dirty whine as we danced together like old friends on the dance floor. I was having so much fun. It seemed like we both desperately needed to unwind and kick back. And Jen could really dance! She rolled her exposed midriff flirtatiously to the beat before dropping into a twerk bounce before bringing it back up and dropping again. I screamed and cheered her on as we high-fived and danced harder.

The crowd must have been feeling our vibe too as they cheered us enthusiastically. The short skirt was a little too short for some of the moves I was serving but I didn't care because I was still dressed more conservatively than Jen, whose ass was literally bursting out of her booty shorts. She took off the sky-high wedges that completed her ensemble and danced barefoot in the sand.

For a moment I thought I lost Jen until I spotted her walking towards me holding two drinks in her hands. *Okay, now! Where did that beach bar come from?* I wondered humorously as I grabbed a drink, and we raised our glasses in 'cheers!' The fruity drink was deliciously deceptive. It was cute and the alcohol was subtle, but it packed a mighty punch from whatever liquor it contained. By the time I finished mine, I felt the rising heat of tipsiness and was totally loose.

Jen turned to me and asked over the loud music, "Hey, that guy the other day... What was the deal with him?"

I shrugged my shoulders in response like I was playing dumb. She didn't buy it.

She squinted her eyes suspiciously and said, "Stop fucking playing with me, Rhi. You know who and what I'm talking about." She chugged the rest of her drink and said, "There was a reason you looked like you wanted to scratch his eyeballs out. Maybe it had something to do with the look he was giving you." She giggled innocently.

"You're tipsy," I said, blowing her off.

"Not yet... but I plan to be in a second," she said and paced to the bar, coming back moments later with two more drinks. She shoved one into my hands and yelled, "Cheers!"

I accepted it gracefully and took a sip of the sweet, tangy concoction.

"*Mr. I Want To Taste Your Bath Water* had you shook the other day, Rhi!" she continued to tease, her words becoming a drunken slur.

I groaned inwardly, closing my eyes slowly and re-opening them to clear some of the haziness from the drink, "Oh. *That* guy."

Jen laughed, "Yeah. *That* guy. Do you two know each other? He's fucking hot!"

I responded saucily, "No, I don't know him, but I know guys like him." I waved a dismissive hand in the air. "Think they're God's gift to the world. Low effort but having women chasing after them like they're the prize. No thank you, ma'am." I threw both hands up, closing them and pulling them in as if I was snatching life itself from the air. "I have no time or patience for that type."

"News flash, Rhi. Apparently *he* didn't get the memo, the way he was checking out your rump shaker? *Mmm...*"

I rolled my eyes and started back dancing. This time, filled with joy juice, my moves became a little bit more fluid, and I lost myself in the beat. Before long, Jen was right beside me bouncing and popping, too.

Chapter 14 - Kendrick

I COULDN'T MISS THAT red hair anywhere, those fiery curls that did a dance of their own. That revealing skirt left her long, thick thighs exposed as she whined her body down to the ground in a move that made my groin tighten. The light of the burning torches lining the dance area of the beach shined off her skin, making her radiate with a glow. She was working it. The short skirt strained as she pushed her ass out before rolling her body up to a sexy standing pose before catching the next beat and bouncing her ass again to the rhythm. *Who is this witch?*

Who knew this tight wad could get this loose? Dancing like she was a teenager at home in front of the mirror. Totally uninhibited. I was mesmerized and only came out of my trance when I heard Micah chuckle. "*Brah*, pick your jaw up and quit drooling," he teased.

I gave him a stony look, which made him chuckle harder. "I've seen that look before, man. It's been a while since I've seen it, but you haven't taken your eyes off her since you spotted her on that dance floor."

I couldn't deny the truth in his statement. Torches were arranged in a small square area near the bar that created the illusion of a dance floor on the beach. The seductive ambiance it created was erotic as fuck. I had to force my attention away from the seductive glow the fire light cast on the dancer's skin. The dancer who had my undivided attention.

Micah and I decided to blow off some steam before the upcoming week, where we would have to immerse ourselves into the hospital cleanup. I didn't know where he got the idea to come down to the beach tonight, but it must have been advertised as the place to be. Tourists from the temples and other nearby attractions were here in droves. It was livelier than I expected, considering the area had been hit by a major natural disaster. But this was Bali. Even still, I didn't expect to see Rhiyan Carson here.

When I looked over at her again, she was enjoying a drink, probably something fruity, with one of the international volunteers I recognized from the school the other day. I could tell Rhi was a bit older than her companion, but the younger woman didn't hold a torch to Rhiyan's grown and sexy curves, or dance moves for that matter. She was stunning and according to Micah, it must have been quite obvious that I wanted her. *Bad.*

The drummer kicked up another party beat and the crowd of dancers, including Rhi and her friend, went into a tizzy. I barely heard Micah holler to let me know he was going to the bar because I was too busy wondering what Rhi was going to do with these two shirtless guys who had sandwiched her between them.

Undaunted, she threw her ass back at one and rolled her chest and shoulders better than Shakira at the other. A pang of jealousy burned my gut when she turned around and dropped it again while sliding her hands down the bare, ripped chest of the lucky fuck who was immediately in front of her. Then she did this little wiggle move with her hips as she brought it back up again.

I'm not exactly sure when my legs began to move across the sand towards her, but by the time Micah was back with the drinks, I was behind her on the dance floor. The beat had changed and the guy who was behind her moved on to dance with someone else. When Rhi turned around to give him a little bit more of her attention, she met my eyes instead of his.

She froze and stared at me through narrowed eyes. Her eyes were a bit glassy, and I could tell she was a little tipsy. Just when I thought she was going to walk off the dance floor or better yet slap my ass, the beat changed again. It was a little slower but had a pulsing baseline. The warm air hung between us for a moment as we studied each other. Risking the actual possibility that she might slap me; I placed a hand on each of her hips and began swaying tentatively to the beat. At first, she hesitated, but eventually acquiesced to the lure of the music and the drinks.

Her tight eyes and shoulders relaxed. She tilted her head to the side and her eyes slowly dipped down my body then back up to my face as if she was sizing me up. *Oh, she is full of liquid courage. Definitely had more than one drink.* The beat picked back up to a sexy reggae tempo. She appeared to get lost in it as she slowly turned, eyes only leaving mine shortly before she dropped low and started throwing her ass back, all the while looking sexily over her shoulder. She was taunting me to a challenge that I accepted. I placed my hands on her round hips and caught her rhythm.

I'm tall but so was Rhi, so it was easy for me to bury my face in her hair and the side of her neck when she stood tall, still winding her body. Her back pressed to my front. She smelled like coconut and lime, and it drove me wild. The beat was slower now, more sensual. Her body easily melted into it, hips snaking and ass rolling into my groin. I whispered into her ear, "The ice queen moves like a sensual goddess."

Unbothered, she kept right on grinding. I was easily losing the battle as my dick strained against her ass. Against my better judgment, I continued to taunt her, "Better be careful before that little ass skirt slides up too high."

Her body tensed a little, but she quickly recovered and started grinding on my dick harder, trying to throw me off my game. And she did just that. The tell-tale sign of my jaw tensing to match the tightness in my groin was evident. She knew what she was doing. Her smirk grew deeper while she continued to look back, eyes locked on mine over her shoulder. She reached an arm up and backwards around my neck pulling me in closer. Her mouth was positioned upwards in the perfect position for a kiss, but she only grazed my lips while aiming a sex-dripped whisper in my ear.

"Your dick is telling on you, Sir."

She released my neck abruptly, bending all the way forward to touch her toes, ass still tight against my crotch. I was fighting a losing battle, but I was able to get the stiffness in my shorts back under control. She must have sensed it because she threw her head back as her body rolled back upright so that she could pivot and face me. By the time she looked up, all she saw was my back walking away towards Micah and my crew.

Micah was standing there, eyes and mouth wide open before he cupped his hand over it and looked at me like I was a fool. I grabbed the beer he was holding out towards me with his other hand and said nothing as I turned coolly back towards the dance floor. I couldn't help but say, "Man, pick up your lip," then I turned the bottle up to take a deep swig.

"She *guh* kill you," he said.

Rhi had already left the dance floor and I didn't want to risk getting stabbed by the daggers I'm sure she would shoot my way.

Still shaking his head, Micah said, "That was a douche move, *braddah*."

I gave him a wounded look, clutching my chest. "Me? Nah, man," I feigned shock.

"Yeah, I'm 100% sure you're a douche. Did you really just leave that beautiful woman on the dance floor?"

I threw my hands up in innocence, knowing full well I had taken the unspoken challenge between Rhi and I back on the dance floor a little too far. But I wasn't willing to tell Micah that the little hammer named Rhi might have had me shook.

Micah chuckled, "Brah, you a fool with it! You never said the other day what was up with you and her. Did you see her again at your resort?"

"Nah, man," I responded. "I haven't seen her at all since the day we went to inspect the school. The two times we met, I got nothing but attitude from her. I half expected her to slap me a moment ago. Don't know what her problem is with me, but I gave her a dose of her own medicine back on the dance floor."

"Hope it doesn't backfire, brah," Micah said as he slapped me on my back, feigning concern for my safety.

Chapter 15 - Rhiyan

*D*ID THIS MOTHERFUCKER LEAVE *me standing here on this dance floor?* I refused to give him the satisfaction of seeing me flustered. I kept it real cute and sashayed off the make-shift dance floor.

By the time I made it back to Jen, she had made another trip to the bar. She handed over another flowery cocktail and said, "If I wasn't convinced before that you two have some type of connection, I'm totally sure of it now. But I'm not sure who just won *that* battle."

Jen's statement stuck with me. I was fuming at the fact that Kendrick left me standing on that damn dance floor, but the more I thought about it, the more her comment about winning and losing a battle with him resonated. He was affecting me in ways I couldn't control.

I wasn't quite sure when I started playing 'Game of Thrones' with him, but I could tell his ass was affected by me, too. *Why was I finding pleasure in this knowledge?* The fact that he was struggling to maintain his self-control on the dance floor only spurred me to apply more pressure. I was ruthless. And I knew it was working because his body language screamed '*Enough!*' and '*Keep going...*' at the same time. His arms became tense, his palms sweaty, and his brow taut. I could tell he was at war with his lust for me.

I could still feel the imprint of his dick on my ass. *Mission fucking accomplished. Ugh! But he still won the battle.* I mentally shrugged off my confused emotions. He was still an antagonizing jerk, and I still wasn't sure why I was taking pleasure in the fact that he would surely be thinking about *me* tonight.

We left the party shortly after. The tropical heat followed me back to my room, overriding the coolness of the clean sheets and the conditioned air. The heat enveloped my body as I envisioned flashbacks of muscled, tattooed arms caressing my waist.

What I imagined his body to look like during our first encounter in the hotel lobby was in plain view on the beach. Kendrick wore Bermuda-styled beach trunks, flip flops, and no shirt. *Damn.* The stiff peaks of his chest and abs were on full display. His arms had to be the size of my thighs, all bulging muscle and rippling tendons. His calves were huge and muscular. *Oh, he worked out...* And not just his upper body like some guys with big chests and skinny legs did.

I stood face-to-face with that chest, and it was impressive. The large pecks molded into rippling abs that tapered into a deep V, disappearing mysteriously into his shorts. At this point, I knew it wasn't the heat of the night that had my brow damp and inner thighs moist. He had gotten to me.

A little embarrassed, I internally winced as it occurred to me that I may have fucked up. The intention was to put the heat on him, but damn if he hadn't unknowingly put it on me. Judging from the bulge I felt through his shorts for that hot second it was pressed against my ass, I could tell he was well endowed. *Oh, my gawd.* The thought of that alone had me throbbing. A cold shower was necessary. This was quickly becoming my normal evening activity where Kendrick Kekoa was concerned.

The next morning, I woke up early and called Danny again to take me to the open-air market that he told me about on the way to Kuta the day before. It was in the opposite direction towards the beach town of Seminyak.

Monday was the big day: the center would be officially open. We already had over 30 children from the local neighborhoods registered. It was going to be hectic but fun. In preparation, I wanted to get fruits and snacks to hand out at the door to make the children feel welcome.

Of course, the local government was providing lunch for the children, some of who were still living in shelters and even missing loved ones in the rubble. My maternal instinct insisted I get some things to make these babies feel special. Just a few things to take their minds off the heartbreak and sorrow that many of them were dealing with.

The open-air market was located just off a long, winding road perched atop a small cliff overlooking the brilliant blue waters of the ocean below. The waters were a magnificent backdrop for the many colorful stalls of everything from fresh fruit, handmade batik scarves, to men making wooden carvings on the spot. There were rows and rows of everything from ornately painted bowls and vases to handmade jewelry and metalworks. The market was open and vibrant and full of beautiful locals selling their wares with tourists like myself spending mini fortunes on the amazing finds.

People were everywhere. It was a bustling area of young boys and girls on skateboards and bicycles. Teenagers and young folks zipped through the streets on mopeds carrying surfboards on their way to and from the beach. Older gentlemen sat at tables playing chess, checkers, and card games, while women in brightly patterned skirts sat at manual looms spinning custom batik fabrics on the fly.

I loved it here. I felt like I found my tribe, fitting right in with my new, yellow one-piece swimsuit and long sarong wrapped around my waist in a makeshift skirt—similar in fashion to the local ladies sitting at the looms.

Every now and then a young lady at the market would ask if she could touch my hair, which I had styled into a thick, cascading mane, pinned back on one side with a decorous accessory painted with seashells that matched the yellow of my swimsuit. Back home I would have been so offended at the thought of some random person asking to touch my hair. In this magical place, I knew it was coming from a place of genuine curiosity since they probably didn't often lay their eyes on people like me. I was cool with it.

I purchased several pounds of fresh fruit and wrapped pastries for the kids. One of the vendors even convinced me to try snake fruit. I was skeptical about trying any fruit that looked like a nut covered in literal snakeskin, but I found the flavor to be somewhere between that of a pear and a plum mixed. It was good and a couple of pounds were added to my ever-growing bag of treats.

I continued up and down each of the rows of stalls in the market and purchased several batik scarves for Jai, Delia, and some of the other ladies in the office as souvenirs. I also bought several pairs of earrings and intricately carved and colored wooden bangles for myself and as gifts, too. I finished off my purchases with a pair of hand-made leather sandals that I would never find back home.

This trip to the market was everything. Even though it wasn't totally the plan, I bought all the souvenirs I needed for everyone on this one trip—including a wooden carving of a dragon for my Dad's ever-growing collection of 'Game of Thrones' collectibles.

I walked around a little bit more before the smells of cooking meat and spices toyed with my senses and my stomach was gurgling with hunger. I stopped at a small open *warung* at the end of one of the back aisles and ordered a noodle bowl. There was a small line, so I placed my order and waited patiently on the side with the other patrons.

"A bit early for you to be out, isn't it?" The hairs on the back of my neck pierced upward at the close proximity of a familiar voice. "The way you were dropping it like it was hot on the beach last night, I'd think for sure you'd be nursing sore muscles and a hangover this morning..." he trailed off as I spun to face him.

"Is this your way of calling me old, Mr. Kekoa?" I said, head tipped to the side as I met his eyes straight on. Again, our faces were barely inches from each other, but I stood my ground, nudging him back a little as I crossed my arms in front of my body to create space. His quick backstep confirmed that I caught him off guard. I continued to stare boldly at him. "Are you following me?"

Ever ready to taunt me, his lips turned up into a wickedly sexy grin, and he responded, "No, I'm not following you, Ms. Rhi." A playful and oh-so-seductive look played at the corner of his eyes. I wanted to slap it off his face because I knew those honey-dipped words would be followed by reckless ones. I pursed my lips and cut my eyes at him, waiting for it.

"As far as you being old," he grabbed his chin and looked up deep in thought then teetered his hands up and down as if weighing his opinion. "Mmm, you were a little stiff on the come up of that last dip you did last night."

And there it was. My arms were still crossed as I rolled my eyes slowly up to the sky, shaking my head in disbelief at the audacity of this prick. He shrugged nonchalantly and continued, "I wouldn't say old, but you definitely don't have Megan's knees."

I struggled to hold back my laugh at the foolishness I knew he'd been crafting in that twisted head of his. Before I could find something slick to say back, the vendor called out that my order was ready.

When I turned around, Kendrick handed me a napkin and plasticware right on cue. He tipped the bib of the U of H hat that covered his bald head, giving me a white-toothed smile and a wink before saying, "Ms. Rhi," and turning to walk away. Again, leaving me speechless, this time with the full view of his backside in the light of the brilliant morning sunlight.

Chapter 16 - Kendrick

AFTER LEAVING THE MARKET, I realized that I was having way too much fun pestering Rhi. After all the attitude she gave me, I made up my mind that she deserved it. Only seemed right in the moment that I antagonized her as payback for her unjustifiable attitude. However, whenever I walked away from her, there was a hint of sadness in her eyes that she'd quickly disguise with a stony look of contempt aimed directly at me. And she left me feeling like the jerk I was being.

Now, don't get me wrong. Ms. Vixen could certainly hold her own, but I felt this huge urge to learn more about her, to be around her even if just for a little while longer.

I knew she probably didn't deserve my harassment, nor was I supposed to be giving her this much of my energy, but she was taking up way too much space in my head, and that was some shit I was not used to. I was Kendrick *fucking* Kekoa, CEO of Kekoa Industries. I did not have the time nor desire to be saddled down by any woman right now. Yes, I had my share of beautiful ladies I spent time with, but none serious enough to occupy more than a fleeting night of fun when I wanted to blow off some steam.

Rhi, on the other hand, stayed ever present on my mind since our first encounter in the hotel lobby when she busted her pretty ass. To make matters worse, every time I'd seen her since then, I wanted to find a way to just stay in her presence. Mad childish, I knew.

There was more to this woman than what met the eye. Aside from her being drop dead gorgeous, that sadness in her eyes juxtaposed with the sassiness in her hips and the bite of her tongue just made me want to get under her skin. However, the apparent disdain she had for me really didn't provide much of an opening for me to even spark up a conversation.

She surprised me last night though. The way she moved her body into mine told a different story about the Ice Queen. Outwardly, she seemed to dislike me. Any hotblooded man could feel beneath the icy surface was a fire that radiated with yearning. There was a longing in the sway of her hips, a void that her body was calling me to fill. That should have spelled trouble, but my dumbass was totally smitten.

Thoughts of how she would feel beneath me had my groin tightening again when the captain's voice cut through my musings as he announced that we were about 20 minutes out from the coast of Lombok, my mother's final resting place. Getting myself together, my thoughts shifted from Rhi to my mother.

I was in the market this morning buying flowers to put out to sea in her honor. It had long been a ritual that I performed every time I came back to Bali and the neighboring islands.

I was only six when I lost her. She'd brought me to Bali with her back in '79 on a mission that she embarked on for *Doctors Without Borders*. She knew I loved the ocean and wanted me to experience the majestic beaches of Bali. I remembered her telling me on the plane ride, "Son, the waters of the Pacific are amazing, but they do not compare to the blue waters of Indonesia." I giggled excitedly as she talked about the color. "It's blue like Jell-O. Pretty enough to take a slice and eat it."

We were here back then under similar circumstances to my visit this time around. A devastating 6.3 magnitude earthquake rocked the Karangasem Regency area of Lombok, killing several hundred people and injuring thousands, toppling buildings just like the one that hit Bali less than a month ago. Back then, there was little to no infrastructure on the islands, and medical care was nonexistent. My mother was a doctor volunteering on a mission to provide medical care to the thousands of injured men, women, and children devastated by the quake.

I thought of my mother's beautiful spirit as the small passenger boat careened over the soft white waves of the expanse of blue water. It saddened me quite a bit, that I ceased to remember the details of her face, but I'd never forget the copper-brown hue of her skin or the golden and reddish highlights of her amazing afro. She was fierce. I always wanted to remember her as a warrior. I thought about how strong she was and how I thought she was a hero back then. She could do no wrong in my wonderous six-year-old eyes.

I often wondered how my life would have turned out had she been alive as I grew into a man. I wondered if she would have liked my girlfriends if I brought them home. I imagined what she would look like now and if she would still be traveling around the world like she did back then. I imagined her eyes lighting up at the sight of her grandchild entering the room.

I don't know when it happened, but my thoughts drifted from my mother back to Rhi's similarly copper toned face. I now wondered what her hair would feel like in my hands as I ran my fingers through it... what her full lips would feel like pressed against mine... what the skin at the nape of her neck would taste like as I smothered it in kisses. True to my lustful, masculine man nature, I daydreamed about what her round ass would feel like as I pulled her into the deep embrace of a passionate kiss.

I groaned and pulled myself out of my reverie. We had arrived. The captain and the small crew were pulling the boat onto the beach. As I jumped over the side of the boat, I was struck with the similarities of my mother and Rhi. Two women on a mission to do some good in this world. Both running away from something. My mother, a loveless marriage. Rhi, I had yet to find out.

Chapter 17 - Rhiyan

IT WAS MONDAY. THE center was finally open! All the snacks were laid out on a welcome table at the entrance. Gro, me, and the four other volunteers stood anxiously waiting at the door for the first bus load of students to arrive.

We were expecting roughly 30 children ranging in age from 5 to 14. So, we had to ensure we could divide them up by age group and activities. Jen and Francis had set up the classrooms with crayons and coloring books for the younger kids. Jeff and Dominic laid out pop culture magazines, pens, and notepads for the older kids.

The excitement was palpable. I was going to be working with the smaller children, the five- to seven-year-olds as each of the volunteers would manage 5 or 6 students similarly grouped by age.

The first bus arrived just after 9 a.m. with roughly ten students. Not as many as we were expecting, but the small group was full of energy. Surprising, considering what they had been through.

Many of them had parents and siblings who were still in the hospital, while a few had lost one or both parents in the rubble.

It was inspiring to see how resilient these kids were. We were all amped to create an experience and atmosphere to give them the space to be kids and take their minds off the devastation for a few hours out of each of their days.

Around mid-day, we gave out snacks to the kids and took them outside to play for a brief recess. The older kids ripped and ran across the grassy courtyard playing tag while the younger kids were jumping rope.

Jen had helped a few of them use sidewalk chalk to draw a hop-scotch board. I was enjoying the sunshine and looking out at the kids from the front door of the school. My focus had been drawn to the building across the street to the men in hard hats that were prying the wood from the boarded-up doorway to gain access. What looked like a glimpse of Kendrick going through the door caught my attention. I didn't realize how much of my attention was across the street until I felt a tug at the hem of my button down.

I looked down to be greeted by Naijah's pink, ruddy cheeks and impossibly adorable eyes. She asked, "What you looking at?" catching me off guard. I glanced back across the street one more time to a now empty entrance to the building. I shook the fleeting image of Kendrick off as a figment of my imagination. I gave my full focus back to Naijah, "*Umm*, nothing cutie."

I pinched her cheek and squatted down in front of her, "Are you enjoying yourself today?"

She grinned broadly and took a small cellphone covered in a pink Hello Kitty stamped phone case and said, "It's great!" Her energy had me giggling so hard and I was even more thrilled to oblige her next request. "Ms. Rhi, can we record a Tik Tok?"

"Absolutely, we can! What do you have in mind?"

She shouted, "Yay!" so loud the other girls all but abandoned the hopscotch game to join me and Naijah as she showed all of us the moves to what she called the breakfast challenge. I must admit, it was amazing. In about 30 minutes, Little Miss Tik Tok Queen had all of us in order shaking our hands, whipping imaginary eggs and eating imaginary corn on the cob over a hip-hop beat. When we finished the last take, she explained to each of us that she was going to post the video as soon as her cellular service worked again.

The first day quickly came to a finish. We were helping the kids clean up the classrooms and get their things together before the bus came to take them all home. Naijah and I had become fast friends. I'd lost count of the times she'd said I looked like Beyoncé throughout the day. Each time I thought about it, I couldn't help to smile. All but laughed out loud a few times as I also thought back to Kendrick's slick comment about my knees being old. *Another thought of his ass? Sheesh.*

Since the opening of the center, the days came and went much like the first. The kids showed up each morning around 9 a.m. By the third day, we had a total of 42 students in attendance. Word was traveling fast and the kids seemed to love it here as much as we enjoyed having them. *I made the right decision to come halfway across the world on a volunteer mission.*

After we'd gotten the kids back on the bus at the end of the first week, Gro asked each of us to stay back for a few minutes. He started by thanking each of us for the hard work we'd put in and to making the first week a success. Then he asked, "I'd *likes* ideas of *yous* to *makes* next couple weeks better?"

Jen chimed in first.

"The kids are doing great. My group seems to be adapting really well." She paused for a beat, face twisting in concern, "A few of them mentioned that they had not seen either a parent or a sibling since they'd been hospitalized with injuries from the quake."

Francis agreed adding, "Yeah, a few of the kids in my group said the same thing."

Jeff added, "How about we plan a field trip and take them to visit the hospital."

Dominic chimed in, "That would be great! We could have them work on hand-made cards and hand deliver them to the patients."

We all were nodding in agreement. Gro volunteered to reach out to the hospital to get clearance for us to go in the next week or so.

The rest of us began getting all the supplies laid out so the kids could begin working on the get-well cards as soon as they arrived on Monday morning.

Chapter 18 - Kendrick

I REACHED FROM UNDERNEATH the pillow crushed against my head to block the brazen sunlight. I felt blindly for my phone to swipe snooze on the alarm. Much like the last three nights, I didn't get any sleep. *Hell*, how could I when visions of her bendy, twisty body were stuck on replay since our first physical contact almost two weeks ago? My dick was constantly on hard at the R-rated film going on in my mind. I tried to play it cool, but it was hard to focus on my priorities. And right now, I needed total focus at the hospital, the biggest part of the rebuild efforts.

I mustered the courage to finally sit up, feet planted firmly on the floor. My eyes were not ready yet to meet the daylight streaming through the wooden slats of the open shutters. I rolled my head from side-to-side to alleviate the stiffness in my neck, flexing my back and shoulders to shake off the soreness from tossing and turning all night. I stood, groaning as I made my way to the shower, hoping the exposure to cold water would shake me fully awake. I needed to be laser-focused today.

We were already working to clear the west annex of the hospital where the trauma team and the bulk of the patients who were injured during the quake were being temporarily housed—since it sustained the least damage in the whole medical complex. We needed to get that wing cleared ASAP to ensure none of the essential workers or patients were placed in further danger. All of the major trauma equipment and beds were moved to this area as well, and we needed to be sure they were safe, too.

The plan wasn't to work in split teams just yet, but if we were going to stay on schedule to start focusing our attention on the east wing, then we'd have to. Since the most damage was on the east wing, if we could split up today, we might be able to finish the hospital restoration early. *This is what I should have been focused on all this time. How could I let myself get so distracted? Why is it such a struggle to stay focused?*

"Ugh," I groaned under the sting of the cool water. I really couldn't afford the lack of sleep right now.

I finally made it to the worksite, slightly groggy and exceptionally irritated. One of my foremen, Ezra, got off on the wrong foot upon arrival. "Man, damn. We're going to be here *all night* if we split up."

I kept quiet and remained focused on the things that weren't going according to plan: the equipment wasn't in place and the rebar delivery was delayed, which would inevitably push back the pouring of the concrete footings in the parking deck. As I felt the heat creep up my neck and across my already tense shoulders, the fool kept right on complaining.

"Phone service not up yet on the westside of the island, so I won't even be able to tell old girl I can't swing through tonight," he muttered just loud enough for everyone to hear him.

That was when I lost it. "Dude, you've only been on site for two hours and you're already complaining." I was in his face before my brain even registered that my feet moved. His nagging mixed with my headache pushed me over the edge. I was about to send his ass back to his room to pack his shit until Micah's quiet demeanor intervened and prevailed. He damn near had to pull me off Ezra's punk ass.

"Yo! Kendrick," Micah spoke up, breaking me out of my red rage. "We got the remainder of the walk through over here…" He threw his arm around Ezra's neck, essentially making himself a human shield around the man before I cold cocked his ass. "Now's as good a time as any to go ahead and split up," he looked at me, eyebrows raised in a way that silently checked my ass into chilling the fuck out. "Why don't we finish up over here and you and the rest of the team go meet with the guys in the east annex?"

I straightened up my stance, nodding at my best friend, knowing full well he was right, and I was dead ass wrong for letting Ezra get under my skin. I took a step back and relaxed my shoulders before giving Micah a fist pound, "Good idea. You, Wren, and Ezra finish up over here. The rest of you, come with me."

My small crew and I left them to it and headed over to the east wing parking decks, which had been beat down and bulldozed so the reconstruction could take place—this time with a custom mix of recycled concrete from the original structure and other mixed materials with Kekoa's patented bonding material. We specialized in sustainable infrastructure design and materials that would keep a good bit of the debris out of the landfills and would also reinforce the structure in a way that allowed it to withstand natural disasters.

The two weeks we were on ground, we had the site cleared and the concrete trucks ready to pour the foundation for the new parking deck. The rebar delivery was going to set our schedule back by a few days, but I had a plan to move us along by redirecting the ground crews to other tasks that had been planned for later.

We still needed to assess the offices, patient rooms, and building systems too, so I sent my small team ahead to do just that. At the same time, I met with Putu, one of the local project managers who was leading the team building the new parking deck.

I met Putu a few years back on another project my team and I led in Bali. He was highly regarded by Ketut, and I'd met his family at one of the many parties hosted by the minister. I trusted his work, so when he reported that the parking decks were going to be completed by the next week even with the rebar delays, I trusted him.

My mind began to wander back to Rhi in the middle of Putu's status update. I had to mentally arm-wrestle my thoughts back to the present as the chirping of my walkie talkie went crazy.

I held up a finger to Putu, "It's Micah. Give me a second to take this." Putu nodded and stepped back to give me privacy.

"Yo, Micah. What's up?" *Chirp.*

"Bruh, I'm getting a weird reading on the seismograph." *Chirp.*

"What do you mean 'weird'? Over." *Chirp.*

"It's probably nothing, but these readings are all over the place. High for a few minutes then low or back to normal." *Chirp.*

"What's the highest reading you're seeing?" *Chirp.*

"3.9 is the highest so far." *Chirp.*

I didn't say so, but the number was pretty high for the readings to possibly be false due to the cranes and heavy equipment movement over at my end. "You're right. It's probably nothing," I said with a chuckle that didn't match the unsettling feeling in the pit of my stomach. "I'm on my way to you in a little bit. I'll check it out once I get there."

I scratched my head after finishing up with Micah, deciding to trust my gut and hurry to go check things out. I walked back over to Putu. "Hey, man... sorry. I had to take that. It's lunch time, go ahead and have your crew break for the day."

"Man, these guys are not going to be so happy with the time off without pay. They've been working hard getting this parking deck back in. You sure you don't want us to start on some of the other work?"

I shook my head. My instincts told me that something was wrong. I didn't want to alarm him, so I kept my voice as calm as possible. "Nah. Forget about it. Matter of fact, have your crew break for the day with pay." I began walking back towards the west annex then paused to turn back to Putu, "I have a few guys on this side doing some additional assessment." I nodded upward at the row of windows over my shoulder, "Can you send someone up to let them know that I said to knock off for the day as well? Y'all get out of here. *Now.*" I realized the order had come out a bit too harsh when I saw him standing there looking at me quizzically. Taking the edge off, I repeated, "Stop working and let everyone know to takeoff, brah."

"Say less, my man," Putu started walking backwards with hands up in a gesture of peace. "No problem at all with the time off with pay." He shrugged off his questions and then turned to hurriedly begin rounding up the crew.

I raced over to the west annex. Doctors and nurses scurried back and forth, analyzing this patient or that, reviewing monitors that blipped and bleeped in an orchestra of technical sound. I almost knocked over a few of the busy workers in my haste and was almost run down by a gurney that came barreling around one corner. There was a nurse sprinting to get a hold of a loud, blaring machine, almost colliding with me and the gurney. It was a chaotic mess. And the chaos quickly elevated my anxiety.

I rounded the final corner where Micah waited for me in one of the less busy waiting rooms. I slowed to catch my breath, but before walking in, I noticed a little girl walking up the hallway. When she turned the corner, I could tell she was totally engaged with the screen of her phone. She seemed naggingly familiar. I wanted to call after her but was pressed to get to the instrument Micah needed me to check.

As I stood there analyzing the numbers, the screen began to glitch and the ground beneath our feet trembled. Micah and I locked eyes; fear evident on our faces.

"You felt that, too?" I asked.

He nodded. "Yeah, that definitely was a tremor, not strong but..." he paused, eyes wide in horror.

The ground began shuddering again. Stronger, this time. Strong enough to send goosebumps up my spine, electrifying the hairs on the entire length of my body.

Micah began moving fast towards the door. "Come on, brah! The kids from the school are visiting today."

That's when it struck me. *I remember that girl... where I saw her... she was one of the kids from the center. Oh, no...* I bolted out the door behind Micah, anxious to find her and get her to safety. She wasn't in the hallway anymore. *Fuck. Why didn't I stop her when I first saw her?* Micah and I decided to split up. My feet propelled me forward at a breakneck speed. Micah sped off in the opposite direction to find the rest of the volunteers and kids from the school.

It was extremely rare to still feel aftershocks several weeks after a quake. This could mean nothing, or it could be another earthquake altogether. A million thoughts were going through my head as my feet moved and my lungs burned. The most pressing task was to find the little girl and warn everyone to evacuate immediately.

It occurred to me that if those kids were here, Rhi most likely was too. The thought of her being in danger fueled my adrenaline. I still didn't wrestle with the feelings that she was stirring in me, but my hands got clammy and my stomach lurched along with the floor and building around me.

Chapter 19 - Rhiyan

"OK, KIDS! LOAD UP," I repeated for the third time as I tried to wrangle them into the waiting van.

Jeff and Dominic were yelling similarly at their groups of horseplaying kids. They were all excited about the field trip. By the way it was going, just getting these kids in the vans, I knew the volunteers and I were going to be run ragged by the end of the day. I pasted a grin on my face to keep the atmosphere light, though. I kept repeating, "Today is going to be a great day" over and over to help me maintain my sanity.

"Alright! Listen up," I yelled, standing at the opening of the bus. "I need everyone to take a seat so I can call roll."

I called out several of the names and marked them present on my log.

"Naijah," I waited, receiving no response.

I thought maybe I just didn't hear her, so I repeated it louder this time.

"Naijah!" again, no response but I was sure I'd seen her get in the van. I began moving towards the back, and suddenly she popped up from behind one of the seats.

"I'm here, Ms. Rhi," she said with a bit of a sheepish grin on her face. "I was watching a Tik Tok on my phone."

"Put your phone away for a minute and listen up to the rest of the announcement so you don't miss anything important," I said, moving to stand in front of her.

She gave me a sweet hug and said, "Yes ma'am."

I rubbed her curly topped head and gave her a high-five before heading back to the front of the van. I finished the attendance and gave a few more instructions to the kids on how they were expected to behave, and we were off.

On the ride, I'd discovered what had her so occupied that she missed her name. She was engrossed in a YouTube video tutorial on the choreography of Beyonce's '*Run the World*' Tik Tok challenge. I sat with her for the rest of the ride, and we watched it together.

Once we arrived at the hospital, each volunteer took charge of their group of kids. Mine were the six and younger kids, including Naijah. We planned the schedule out meticulously so each of the four groups would visit four patient rooms each, then we'd all meet back up in the cafeteria for lunch before heading back to the center.

"Ok, *mon petites*," Dominic spoke in French to his group of tweens. "Let us hurry and give out all of the cards. I'm starving!" He received ruckus laughter from his group as they all walked in a huddle toward their first patient room.

That was the rest of our queue to follow suit. Each group went in four different directions. Armed with the list of patients' names and room numbers that my group of six would visit, we made our merry way to our first patient, an elderly gentleman with the kindest eyes. He was thrilled to see the children and happened to be the grandfather of one of the little boys in my group, Gede. He barely spoke English, but Naijah translated for me.

He reached for his grandson, who quickly climbed up on the bed to sit by his Papa. In his native tongue, he said, "Come, come," holding his arms out wider.

That's all it took and each of the remaining kids all jumped up on the bed and took turns reading and giving him the cards they'd made for him in class. He accepted each graciously, a pool of grateful tears teetering in the corners of his eyes. He nodded a silent thank you to me before regaling the group with a story about the moon goddess, *Dewi Ratih,* and how her beauty was so desired that she was swallowed whole by another deity but she was able to escape through his neck. *Okay, this story turned left real quick.* At any rate, the brief darkness caused by her absence was the manifestation of what we know as a lunar eclipse. The kids loved the story and a few of them seemed to know it already. I was beginning to realize that the Balinese people worshipped many deities and the culture was steeped in mythology. I'd heard about several from Danny as he pointed out statues of some of them on our last outing.

We stayed a few extra minutes to hear the story 'til the end. I was enjoying the smiles on their faces just watching them.

We made our way to visit the next three patients, each visit much like the last. The children presented their cards, and the patients smiled or teared up with joy from their thoughtfulness. It turned out that there were a couple more of the patients that at least one of the kids knew. This made the trip that much more special because a lot of them had not seen family members and loved ones since the day of the earthquake. It was like bringing a small family reunion to their hospital beds.

We were on the way to our fourth and final patient's room, and the day was going off without a hitch. We were walking down a longer corridor. It seemed like there was more medical activity there. I kept the kids in a single file line towards the right of the hallway so as not to impede the heavy foot traffic.

All of a sudden, I seemed to lose my footing and had to grab the wall for balance. One of the passing doctors looked at me in concern, and I shook it off casually, keeping the small group moving. Then it happened again. This time, one of the nurses also stumbled. Both of us kept our footing, but it was all strange, nonetheless.

As I was turning to let the kids know that I was fine, I felt butterflies in my stomach as a sense of vertigo came over me. I felt like my feet were on a swaying ship; the weightless effect of my body made me feel nauseous. At first, I thought I might have had something going on with my inner ear, perhaps a result of my morning swims in the ocean. However, that didn't explain why the nurse also lost her footing or why all the of the doctors and nurses congregating in the hallways were saying they felt the same thing. Something was wrong.

"Everyone let's hold hands," I said to the kids who were now starting to look frightened. "Change of plans. Let's go find the others and have lunch a bit earlier!" That cheered them up a bit.

I remained calm for their sake; it seemed to be working. We turned to go back in the direction that we had come. When we got back to the central desk area near the entrance of the hospital, I realized that I only had five of the six children there holding hands.

"Where's Naijah?" I asked, starting to panic for the first time. They all looked at me now, eyes big with fear.

"I don't know," they said simultaneously and shrugged their tiny shoulders.

Naijah had fallen behind the group a couple of times while on her phone, but I was able to get her to hustle and catch up. This time, I didn't see her when I looked back down the corridor. My heart was starting to beat through my chest when I saw Jeff and his group come around the corner.

"Oh my God, Jeff. I'm so glad to see you!" I called nearly out of breath as I rushed the group of kids over to him. "I think I just felt the building tremor, and one of my kids is missing."

"We felt it, too," he stated calmly, his eyes betraying the fear he felt.

I'm sure the emotion was mirrored on my own face, but I didn't confirm the thought out loud for fear of scaring the children any more than they already were.

"Get the kids back to the vans," I ordered. "I'm going to go find Naijah." I didn't stick around to hear his response before I dashed back down the corridor.

I fought my way through a crowd of doctors, nurses, and some patients and stopped only briefly to ask if they had seen a little girl wandering the hallway. They all said 'no'. I sped up my pace peeking into each room as I made it to the end of the hallway.

I made a right turn and continued my frenzied search. More doctors and nurses. Again, I asked, "Have you seen a little girl? She's six and about this tall..." I placed my palm next to my waist, indicating Naijah's approximate height, "with a pink Cocomelon book bag on, probably glued to her phone." More shrugs and I-don't-knows. I was out of breath from moving so fast but wouldn't slow my pace down the hallway except when stopping to look in each of the rooms.

The floor lurched again. This time hard enough to make me lose my balance. I used both hands to break my fall and faintly felt a sharp stab of pain in my palm. I dismissed it and kept moving. I had to find Naijah. Images of the little girl in the picture right after the first earthquake spurred me on.

Many doctors, nurses, and patients who were able to walk were speedily going past me in the other direction. Others were being pushed in wheelchairs towards the exits. Some were running, some walking very fast, but all were trying to get out of this building. In passing I heard a scared nurse say, "Is it happening again?" more as a statement than a question.

I knew the "it" she was referring to was another earthquake. That made me move faster, lungs now burning, I pushed through to find this little girl. I was quickly coming to the end of the hallway cursing aloud. She couldn't have made it this far, I thought frantically, stopping to place my hands on my knees, sucking in air as I decided which way to go. Frustrated, I looked into the last door on the right which was an empty waiting room. Just as I was about to turn to leave, a small movement in the back corner caught my attention. A small, pink bookbag attached to a small child, arms hugging her knees tightly to her chest as she rocked in fear.

"Naijah!" I sobbed in relief. "There you are. I've been looking all over for you!"

I ran to her, arms outstretched.

"Ms. Rhi," she cried, jumping up from her crouched position then rushing to me. I swept her up into my arms as we both cried aloud. "I was so scared. I couldn't find anyone," she sobbed through her tears.

I hugged her so tight, I felt her little heart beating into my chest.

"*Shhh*, it's okay," I comforted her repeatedly.

I put her back on the ground.

"Take my hand! We have to get out of here now… and I need you to run, baby. Can you do that for me?"

She nodded and grabbed my hand. As we exited the waiting room and started running back towards the main entrance, the floor seemed to completely give way. Naijah's hand slipped out of my grasp. I felt her body go one way as a ripple in the floor threw me in the other direction.

I quickly made it to my hands and knees, scrambling towards Naijah. Just as I reached for her, I felt a crack and a sharp pain explode in the crown of my head. And then blackness.

Chapter 20 - Rhiyan

BLINDING SUNLIGHT STOPPED ME from opening my eyes fully. The warm rays felt good on my face. A stark contrast to the coldness of the hospital. *Wait... the hospital. I should be in the hospital with the children!* The thought made my eyes pop open wide, and I fought to get up off the ground but there seemed to be a force pushing me back down. I felt two strong hands keeping me firmly pinned to the ground. My head ached and a wave of dizziness washed over me as I tried to fight free.

"Be still, Vixen," he said close to my ear. "Let the doctors check you out."

"Check me out?" I stammered, not understanding. "I'm fine! I need to go back in and get Naijah," I half yelled, half moaned while making another attempt to free myself from his grip.

"The children are fine, Rhi. Naijah is fine," he soothed. "You got her out of that break room and saved her life. She didn't have a single scratch on her. You, on the other hand, finally got hit upside that pretty head of yours. So *please*, let the doctors finish checking you out," he implored.

His comment reminded me of what he said in jest back at the school. Now was not the time for humor. I fought against his hands again, this time freeing myself just enough to twist my shoulders towards him and tell his ass off. Catching him off guard, he loosened his grip on my shoulders, allowing me to angle my face in the direction of his voice.

Brown eyes locked on brown eyes. I stopped struggling to break free. I expected to find his arrogant eyes mocking me, but behind the sunbathed golden flecks of his irises, I found only genuine concern. It unnerved me. Yet, I couldn't look away.

Neither of us spoke but the stare down communicated volumes. Mine was challenging, writing blank checks I knew I couldn't cash. His appeared to be searching mine for answers—answers I didn't know the questions to. It felt like we stayed this way for a long time. I succumbed to the dull ache at the base of my skull, having no choice but to relax onto his thigh pillowing my head. As I recovered a bit from the wave of dizziness, I realized just how close my face was to the apex of his groin. That should have scared me shitless, pissed me off even. Strangely, it didn't.

The clearing of the nurse's voice broke the trance that Kendrick and I both must have been in. I felt his weight shift as he straightened away from me to focus on what she was saying. Kendrick's presence was so consuming, I forgot for a moment that I was being examined. Embarrassed, I angled back in the direction of the hand that still lingered on my left shin.

"You're going to be just fine. I didn't find anything other than that nasty cut and the knot on your head," the doctor reassured.

I held up my hand, realizing the bandages for the first time.

"Does she have a concus-"

"What about the pain in-" Kendrick and I said simultaneously.

Again, our eyes locked. This time his head angled down towards mine.

"I'm sorry," he said, maintaining the eye contact. "The lady was saying?"

It was hard to pull my attention away from his sexy, low voice.

"My head," I tried again, looking back towards the nurse.

"What about the pain? It's not serious, is it?"

"No. Nothing too serious. We've ruled out a concussion," she said, this time eyes on Kendrick. "But she may have a bit of pain at the site of where she was struck. Just keep an eye on your..." her words began to trail off as she pinned him with a questioning look, "girlfriend?"

We both vehemently shook our heads in unison with a resounding, "No." Kendrick continued, "Ms. Carson is a..." now his words trailed off, "a friend."

"Ok," she said, eyes shifting between Kendrick's and mine before she addressed me. "Take a few days off. You've had a pretty good shake up. Allow your *friend* to take care of you for a few days."

I nodded but wasn't sure how to feel about the way she stressed the word *friend.*

She straightened to leave and patted my leg, "You're pretty lucky this guy was able to carry you out of the building when he did," she gave a wink of approval at Kendrick. "I think you'll be in good hands with this guy." She reached into her pocket to pull out a small envelope and handed it to Kendrick. "I can only give you a few of the pain meds that I was able to snatch on the way out of the trauma center, but they should help with your headache."

She handed me two to take right away, and Kendrick magically handed me a bottle of water that seemed to appear from out of nowhere. The nurse walked away, vanishing into the crowd of waiting patients, leaving us alone.

"Let's get you out of here," he said as he lifted my head gently off his thigh so he could come to a crouching position. He cradled my head in the crook of one arm and slid his other arm under my knees, yanking me up in a single thrust like I was a feather.

The pain meds were already kicking in, so I didn't put up any fight, allowing my cheek to rest against his chest as he carried me in the direction of the open parking lot. The pain was subsiding quickly. *Shit.* I see why people get addicted to pain meds, I was extremely relaxed. The happy pills had me feeling... languid, for lack of a better word.

I held on a bit tighter to Kendrick's neck. I could feel the soothing rhythm of his heartbeat through his chest and the warmth of his skin as he pressed me to his body. I closed my eyes and just listened, hating it when we got to the truck. He somehow was able to unlock and maneuver the door open with me still in his arms. I felt cold when we finally broke body contact, and he placed me gently in the backseat.

"Rhi, can you stay awake for me until I get us back to the resort?" he asked, palm gently cupping my face. I stared at the lips that were again way too close to mine. Lifting my eyes to his, I nodded slowly as my cheek tingled from the sensation of his hand there. He hesitated for a brief moment before reaching to secure the seat belt around me and close the door. He climbed into the driver's seat, and it wasn't long before we were pulling into the gates of our resort.

After checking in with the guards, Kendrick's walkie talkie chirped. My thoughts lingered on the fullness of his lips, so I barely heard the conversation he was having with Micah. Something about a couple of days off... she's good... take care of the men...

In the next moment, the staff at the resort were helping us out of the truck, and someone must have valeted it for us.

Chapter 21 - Kendrick

BEFORE WHISKING RHI TO her room, I stopped at the front desk to ask for a duplicate key card. She was out of it, so I knew it was pointless to ask her to pull hers out. They surely felt the small earthquake over here as well, so there were no questions asked about Rhi's condition or why I needed them to produce a key card to open her room.

I made arrangements for room service to be brought up to the room as well. The 3.5 quake happened just before noon, and it was now almost 4:00. I knew from the other volunteers that they had not had a chance to eat lunch. She'd be starving once the pain meds subsided. I was starving *now*. The problem was that I wasn't sure if it was only for food.

I don't know what shifted in her. Maybe it was the pain meds that had her studying my features from the backseat. She couldn't see me watching her, but I could see the glances she made in the rear-view mirror. Before that, I even felt her hardened nipples pressing into my chest as I carried her to my truck. I almost lost control and kissed her while getting her settled in the backseat. My saner self stopped me and propelled me into that damned driver's seat.

In no time, I got us settled into her room. Just in time for the pain meds to fully kick in.

"*Mmm*," Rhi moaned as she started stripping off her clothes.

"Whoa, Vixen. What you doing?" I said, placing my hand over hers to keep the t-shirt from taking the same path as the pants that were now pooling around her ankles.

She said something unintelligible as she stumbled the few steps to the bed, falling in a heap dangerously close to the edge.

The teal lace of her panties barely covered her beautiful ass. I willed my dick down as I commenced the task of getting her tucked into the bed. I grabbed her ankle and gently stretched her from the fetal position she landed in, gently shifting her towards the middle of the bed where I covered her 'mummy' style in the white sheets.

To create some much-needed distance, I opened the patio doors and waited on the balcony for the food that came shortly after. I ordered a salad and a sandwich for Rhi and something a bit more satisfying for me along with a bottle of Cabernet. After placing her share in the fridge for keeps while she slept, I took mine back out to the balcony, enjoying what turned out to be a beautiful afternoon.

It wasn't until I heard a noise in the inner sanctum of Rhi's room that I realized I'd fallen asleep, too. It was dark out now. I jumped up to check that she was okay.

The room was alive as candlelight danced on the dark walls. But there was no sign of Vixen. I heard the shower turning off, and the door to the bathroom opened. Rhi walked out naked, oblivious to my being in the room.

I cleared my throat and she jumped, startled. I rushed to her, placing my hands on both arms to brace her.

"I'm sorry, I didn't mean to frighten you."

"Kendrick," she stammered. "I thought you'd left." She was visibly shocked to find me in her room but made no effort to move away from me or cover her dripping wet body. She was completely naked, except for the towel around her hair.

I averted my eyes and stepped back.

"I'm sorry. I fell asleep outside and rushed in when I heard you in the shower," I reached up to rub the back of my head to steady my thoughts as I made a move past her to get to the door. "I'll give you some privacy," I said, averting my eyes. I stopped at the sound of her soft voice.

"I must have been out of it. I don't remember much after we pulled up to the resort."

"Yeah. You passed out as soon as we made it to your room. I didn't want to leave you in here alone," I shrugged. "Following the doctor's orders... Anyway, I should go." As I made my way to the door, I felt a hand grasping my bicep timidly.

"Don't go," she whispered. I turned to find her eyes on mine in the candlelit room. I struggled to read the emotion in her eyes, so I didn't move towards her. We stood there in silence for what seemed like ions before she reached out her hand again. My feet moved and I stood directly in front of her.

"Rhi," I whispered. "You sure?"

Her eyes now burned into mine.

"I don't know. I'm fine," she looked away, grappling with her nerves before bringing her eyes back to mine. "I don't want to be alone."

I pulled her to me, curling her close to my chest, simultaneously pulling the towel from her wet hair. The thick wet curls cascaded over her shoulders as a single rivulet of water slid down over a puckered nipple. I closed my eyes momentarily to gain control before asking her again, "Are you sure?"

She gave a single, quick nod, and I bent my head to catch the droplet with my tongue. I lifted my face back up to hers, licking her soft lips, coaxing them open with my tongue. Her lips tasted of cool mint; the recess of her mouth was warm and soft as I explored her tongue and lips.

Her body pressed against mine and she deepened the kiss. I gently pulled away and bent again to find the stiff peak of her nipple, sucking it into my mouth. Her head dropped back, and she moaned again softly as she offered the perfect orbs to me.

"Kendrick," she whispered, allowing my name to drip from her lips followed by a throaty moan that she couldn't control. I cupped her other full breast in my hand and sucked the nipple of that one between my lips as well, continuing to slide the roughness of my tongue over it. I used my other hand to grip her firm ass cheek, crushing her body even closer to mine as both of her arms wrapped around my neck for balance and her back arched, giving me better access to both breasts.

I released her for a moment then hooked my forearms behind her knees, lifting her. She wasted no time and wrapped her legs around my waist so she wouldn't fall. "I got you," I reassured as I carried her to the bed resuming my assault on her large areola, tugging on it with my lips until she moaned again as I gently laid her on the bed.

Chapter 22 - Rhiyan

KENDRICK RELEASED MY NIPPLE and stood looking down at me, wasting no time discarding his shirt. He unbuckled his belt and released the button and zipper of his pants, stepping out of them but kept on the boxer briefs that hugged his huge thighs.

I slid back to the center of the bed, taking the sight of him in, and when I couldn't handle the wait any longer, I reached for him. He didn't hesitate to place a crushing knee on the mattress and move his body up the length of the bed to settle on his side and pull me to him.

He rolled onto his back, pulling me on top and guided my mouth back to his. My nipples ached against the hardness of his chest and my pussy began to throb against the length of his swollen dick. Were it not for his cotton briefs, he'd already be inside me. I ached for this man, a man whose sight I could barely stand less than a week ago. I wasn't sure what propelled me to ask him to stay, but it was undeniably the effect he had on me. Our connection was palpable, and I brazenly wanted him.

He continued to ravage my mouth as I moved my hand between us to stroke his massive dick through his underwear. I broke my lips free from his and nearly begged, "Kendrick, please take these off."

He placed a hand around my wrist, removing it from between us and bringing it up to his mouth, slowly sucking each of my fingers as he pressed me against his body with his other arm, holding my eyes in a smoldering gaze. His slow sucking made my mouth water. I wanted him inside of me; but I also wanted to taste *him* in the same way he tasted and sucked each of my fingers.

"Kendrick, *please*, take these off," I again begged.

He caught me off guard when he flipped me over, now hovering over me before leaving the bed to do as I asked. He slowly pulled the band down, and his dick sprang out pointing directly at me. Before he could move back to the bed, I rose to my knees and crawled to the edge right in front of him.

I looked up into his eyes as I slowly wrapped my lips around the head of his hard dick and sucked him slowly into my mouth. This time his head fell. "*Ahh, Vixen,*" he moaned, nearly losing his balance from the heat of my wet mouth. My pussy got wetter with each of his deep moans. He gained control and began stroking my mouth slowly with his dick until he could barely take it, pulling himself from my grip.

He gently pushed me backwards. "Lay back and open for me, Rhi."

I did as he said and almost lost it when he dropped to his knees, pulling me and my pussy to the edge of the bed to meet his waiting mouth and tongue. I sucked in a deep breath and released it in a shuttering moan of pure pleasure; he wasted no time covering my throbbing clit with his mouth. He suckled my clit and somehow simultaneously dipped his pointed tongue deep into the recesses of my pussy.

"Oh, my God, Kendrick," I cried through my moans. "It feels, *ah-maz-ing*." My back arched, and I spread my legs wider to give him better access. Much like he did to my nipples, he slid the roughness of his tongue over my swollen labia, then inserted two thick fingers inside my wetness.

"Silky," he said on a sex dripped moan as he pumped his fingers in and out of me, sending sweet heat rippling through my core. I panted as waves of an uncontrollable orgasm gripped my body causing my pussy to spasm around his fingers.

The white heat of my orgasm turned into a slow burn as he kept licking and sucking my clit. My head was spinning, my ears ringing. But I didn't want him to stop. I placed my hand on his forehead and pushed him gently away, whispering, "I want to taste me on your lips."

Again, he moved up the bed and I pulled his face to mine to lick my sweet saltiness before pulling his thick lower lip between my teeth.

"*Mmm*," he groaned, pulling me in closer, parting my lips with his tongue. It was an animalistic, hungry kiss, making me want him back in my mouth. "Lay on your back," I commanded, and this gentle giant did as I asked again. Before his back hit the pillows I covered the swollen head of his dick with my lips, sucking and swirling my tongue around the sensitive area just under the mushroomed cap before slowly taking all of him in my mouth this time. "Fuck," he cursed as both of his palms gripped the sheets. "You're going to make me... *ah*..." he groaned.

I slid my lips back up to the tip before taking him in deep again. This time the head of his dick was pressing into the opening of my throat. His breath was coming faster now as he heaved over a low guttural moan that rumbled deep in his chest. I used everything from my neck, tongue, lips, throat, and spit to keep him moaning. That shit turned me on even more.

I felt his inner thighs begin to tighten, and he began to thrust himself deep into my mouth. I kept sucking. In. Out. Hands pumping up and down in steady movement, loudly slurping and not giving a fuck about the wet mess I was making.

"Come here, Rhi," he said, grabbing under my shoulders and sliding me up his body to straddle him. He slid his dick inside me—needing no hands to do so—and pulled me forward, taking my nipples into his mouth one at a time.

He held my hips steady as he slammed up into me with deep, fast strokes hitting my spot with every thrust. He was so hard and so deep, I could barely breath. I didn't care. The pleasure he was giving every inch of me superseded breath in that moment.

He released my hips and we rocked together, faster, both of us needing a release that only the other could give at this very moment. I held on to his forearms, throwing my head back in pleasure. "*Ahh*," I panted, moving my hips faster as I cried, "I'm *cumming*." He kept fucking me, and then I felt his dick pulsating from the base to the head.

"*Fuck*," ripped from his lips as he let go, all control lost as he came, pulsating deep inside of my still throbbing pussy. I collapsed onto his chest. Neither could say a word. He wrapped his arms around me. We lay there. Him, breathing deeply. Me, pressed tight to his chest, breathing in his warm, cocoa buttery scent.

The room was quiet except for the crashing sound of the waves on the cliffs below the room. His breathing was steady, but I could tell he wasn't asleep. I moved to his side and snuggled beside him. He broke the silence, "Are you okay?"

"Yes," I nodded in the darkness. "We didn't use any protection.

"We didn't," he stated.

"I can't have children."

He didn't respond just squeezed me tighter to his chest. We laid this way until we both dozed off to sleep.

Chapter 23 - Kendrick

THE EARLY MORNING SUN escaped through the patio doors that neither of us had the energy to close before drifting off into a sex-hazed slumber. It had been a long time since I spent enough time in a woman's bed to see the sun come up. It had been too often a one-night stand where I'd be up and out of the way before sunrise.

One, because I'd never wanted to miss the breakfast routine of pancakes and sausage with Jada. Two, because I never made myself available for more than a few hours here and there for drinks, maybe a dinner date and a quick hour or two of mutual fun in the sack. As soon as any of the women got a little too clingy, I'd give them the same scripted speech, "Baby girl, I'm not ready for anything long term. I thought we were just having fun."

This morning was different. I was in no hurry to dip out of her room. I was content watching the peace on her face while she slept. She was stunning. Caramel-dipped skin covered her delicate features. The lids of her almond-shaped eyes hid reddish amber orbs that seemed to glow with a fire lit from within. Her nose was neither small nor big but perfectly accentuated the fullness of her lips—which I recently confirmed really were as soft as they looked. Her tangled mass of coils framed her face and cascaded over the pillow, a tell-tale sign of our fuck-fest the night before. My hand moved on its own accord to touch it and tuck a tendril behind her ear.

She stirred and slowly opened her eyes. My fingers grazed her ear softly as I released her hair and brought my hand to rest between us.

"Good morning, beautiful," I said, voice just above a whisper.

We were face-to-face; her sleepy gaze locked on mine. She didn't speak. Vulnerability flashed briefly across her face, but there was no sign of regret over our lovemaking last night. I pulled her close to me and kissed her on the forehead before she buried her face into my chest. We lay this way for a few moments before she swung her feet to the floor. She stood and walked purposefully to the bathroom. Still naked. "I have to pee," she tossed over her shoulder with a shy smile.

While she was in the bathroom, I grabbed my phone and made a quick call to Micah. I asked him to take charge of the crew today, to get a full assessment of the new damage, and keep the east annex work on track. Before disconnecting, I asked him to get word over to the school that Rhi was going to be out for a couple of days per the doctor's orders, but that she was okay, just shaken up a bit. As I hung up, Rhi was emerging from the bathroom, towel wrapped around her body.

She walked over to one of the dressers; after pulling out a swimsuit, she walked back to me. I was on my feet behind her before she had the chance to dress; I tugged the towel, letting it fall to her feet. I pressed my nakedness to her backside and cupped her breasts while kissing the nape of her neck. She moaned as I cupped her breasts and her nipples sprang to life. I could tell her wall was starting to come back up and I needed to interject before we were back to the cold war. I grabbed her and turned her around to face me. She averted her eyes. I cupped her chin, enticing her eyes to land on mine. "No, sweetheart," I whispered. "We are not going back to that again."

I could tell that she was struggling with something, so I kissed her lips and released her. Not wanting to press. At least she didn't pull away. "Get dressed, sexy," I said lightly in her ear.

She hesitated like she was torn between staying in my arms or getting dressed. I was a bit disappointed that she opted for the swimsuit, pulling it over her ass and up around her waist. Again, not wanting to press or make the situation awkward, I helped her pull the straps up over her shoulders, before turning away to grab my briefs and pants.

"So, what are we about to get into?"

"I am going down to the beach to get my daily swim in." She walked past me, tossing a devilish glance my way as she grabbed a beach bag from the closet, checking the contents then donning a pair of YSL shades.

I stood there amused. I was enjoying her playful energy and glad that the full-fledged Ice Queen didn't make a comeback.

"Coming?" she asked.

"Yes. If you allow me to grace you with my company," I said. "Whatever you want to do, Vixen, I'll be right here with you for the next three days. Doctor's orders."

"Right," she said, rolling her eyes. "Doctor's orders."

"You're not going like that, are you?" she flicked an elegant wrist towards my bare chest and jeans.

"If my dick wasn't glued to my leg," I joked, "I would. I just need to run to my room and grab some trunks. Follow me?"

She nodded. I pulled my Polo over my head and slid my socks and shoes on. She grabbed my outstretched hand, and we left her room and rode the elevator up to the top floor.

"Penthouse. Figures," she said dryly. "If arrogant and over the top was a person..."

"Hate doesn't look good on you, Vixen," I smirked, walking into the grand living room of my suite. There was no need for doors as my keycard granted access to the well-appointed suite, courtesy of Ketut.

"I'll just be a minute," I stated as I walked to the bedroom to change, leaving Rhi to peruse the opulent suite. I heard her say, "Damn, this is nice," before I rounded the corner into the room.

I freshened up in the en-suite bathroom. When I emerged, I had my beach trunks on, my chest was bare, and I was sporting casual flip flops and a towel around my neck. I twirled my compressed t-shirt in my hand contemplating putting it on but decided to hand it over to Rhi along with my wallet, pointing innocently to her bag. My puppy-dog eyes said: *"Hold onto these for me, pretty please?"*

She smiled, giving me a quick, "Sure. Why not?" and stowed them both before taking my outstretched hand. Admittedly, I liked the thought of us looking like a couple as we made our way down to the beach.

Chapter 24 - Rhiyan

I watched Kendrick as he walked out of the water towards the semi-private cabana where I was relaxing on one of the shaded lounge chairs. I openly admired his muscular chest, allowing my eyes to roam a bit further down his hard abs to the deep sexy V that disappeared into the waistline of his wet, clingy swim trunks. I completed my swim routine and made it back to the shore before he did. Not because I was faster. He turned out to be a much better swimmer than me. His powerful arms cut through the incoming waves effortlessly. It was breathtaking just watching him.

"I *needed* that swim," he stated, plopping down and straddling the lounge chair beside me. "Been here almost a month this time, and this is the first time I've had any time to enjoy the water." *This time?*

"You seem to know what you're doing out there," I said, gesturing with my chin towards the water. "Impressive."

"You seem surprised," he said with a wounded expression. "I'll have you know, I have years of practice shredding waves much bigger than these."

"Ok, big boy," I threw up my hands in defense, making no effort to hide my amusement from getting under his skin.

Deep in thought, he looked out towards the coastline. "Back home, I'm rarely without my long board whenever I have free time."

"Where is home?" I asked, realizing I never really pondered the origins of his accent or lack thereof. His bronzed skin was dark, almost as dark as mine. Yet, I couldn't decipher his ethnicity. No hair. No hints. I surmised that he must have been from the States because his English was impeccable. "Let me guess, Cali boy," I stated confidently.

"Nah," he looked at me sideways with a comical scowl. "A little further west."

"Further west than Cali?"

Seeing my hiked brow, he stated, "Hawaii. Waikiki born and bred."

That explained the tattoos. I first noticed them that day in the lobby. Too bad I was too wrapped up in his arrogance to pay more attention then. I was able to see them better now. Tribal flames, flowers, and a series of names interwoven into an intricate story across his upper back and down the entirety of one arm.

"*Mmm*," I stated. "Your hair gave it away." I chuckled at my own joke. Laughing deeply, he lifted a chiseled bicep, hand rubbing his bald head. "The ice maiden has jokes, I see."

"Ice Maiden, *huh*? Sooo unoriginal," I teased, my mouth twisting as I gave him the best side-eye I could muster.

"Better than mean girl," he muttered under his breath.

"You mutherfu-" I gave an exaggerated gasp before laughing again at his silliness.

He chortled, ducking swiftly to avoid the faux gesture I made to smack him upside his head.

"I'm not mean," I said, leveling my eyes on him coolly. "I just know your kind."

"And what's my kind, Vixen? Come on with it."

"*Mmm*," I said as if in deep thought. "God's gift to the world. Get into any panties you want. *Love 'em, leave 'em,* and *gaslight 'em* with just enough promise in your kisses to keep hope alive that you can run in and out of that revolving door of pussy whenever you want." I turned and pinned him with my gaze, brows arched high and smiling sweetly at him.

"Damn," he said, looking wounded all over again. "That was very... specific." He allowed an impregnated pause to linger. "Who hurt you? Want me to fuck him up?"

We both burst out laughing again. "Shut up, silly," I said, this time swatting his huge chest in a playful tap.

I turned back towards the ocean, smile faltering a bit. I admired the sparkling, Bali blue water. He was right. My assessment of him was pretty specific, and I was unfairly projecting my own experiences on him again. I got the sense he really wasn't that guy. I was really enjoying our easy banter and his company.

He laid out fully on the lounge now, eyes closed, giving me the opportunity to study him. Aside from the body of an Olympian, he was beautiful in a rugged sort of way. His heavy brow made him look menacing, but the smile that softened the chiseled jawline beneath his perfectly trimmed goatee and those dazzling white teeth did something to me. It had my uterus doing summersaults; pussy doing back flips and pirouettes in my panties. *It should be a sin to be this fucking good looking.*

I was so busy studying his mouth I didn't notice his attention back on me until he reached towards me and trailed the back of his hand over my cheek. Our loungers were close enough that if he craned his neck in my direction his lips would touch mine. He didn't immediately move, but his eyes pierced mine as he languidly said, "You remind me of someone... not physically. I mean, aside from the wild, thick hair... but your tenacity and desire to give of yourself to make the world a better place."

Who? I wondered but didn't ask aloud.

"It came to me yesterday when you were hurt, how similar the two of you are. Were." He wiped a hand over his face almost like he was wiping the memory of something deep from his conscience.

"She must be pretty special," was all I could think to say. The faraway look in his eyes carried a bit of melancholy. I sat there and just listened.

"She died here," he stated, closing his eyes briefly and turning away to break our eye contact. When he turned back to me, his mood had shifted again, and his dazzling smile was back. "Let's get out of here. I'm starving!"

I was taken aback by the sudden change in demeanor. He squinted devilishly and sexily asked, "Are you hungry, Rhi?" Before I could respond, he growled, "Bring your sexy ass here," pulling me in one swift yank from my lounger right on top of him on his.

I put up no fight since we were nearly isolated from the wandering eyes of others on the beach. It surprised me how at one moment I was studying him discreetly—or so I thought—to studying him from a position of dominance on top of him. Up close and personal.

After our love making last night, I wasn't surprised at all that his strong ass could handle me so expertly. I grabbed his bottom lip between mine, gently licking its saltiness and instantly felt the swell of his dick between us.

"*Mmm*," he groaned, grabbing the back of my neck and pulling me in for a punishing kiss that had me ready to pull the crotch of my swimsuit to the side and free the length of him from his wet swim trunks. I moaned into his mouth in memory of his thickness sliding between my wet folds last night, causing me to press my clit into the hard bulge.

Thank God for that tiny strip of polyester being in the way because I wasn't sure I'd be strong enough to not ride his dick right here and now in the cabana.

"I want you, Rhi," he said, releasing my swollen mouth.

Squeezing my eyes shut I responded, "I want you, too, Kendrick. But not here, baby."

I pulled away from him enough to straddle his waist and push myself up into a seated position. We were still pelvis to pelvis as I looked down at him, "What are you doing to me?"

"I don't know. But whatever it is, you're doing it to me, too."

I squealed when he placed his hands firmly under my butt and held me against him as he stood up. I wrapped my arms tightly around his neck from fear of falling. I was amazed at his ability to lift me so effortlessly. He stepped over the lounge and put me down. Then offered his hand. "Let's go eat."

Chapter 25 –Kendrick

"**G**O SOMEWHERE WITH ME."

The words tumbled from my mouth before my brain could stop them.

Her eyes narrowed suspiciously as she held the coffee cup's edge between her parted lips. She seemed pensive for a moment and then proceeded to take the sip, offering a tentative smile and acquiescent nod at my request. *By God, why is it so hard for me to read this woman?*

We finished up our breakfast not ready to part ways. I didn't think it all the way through and wasn't quite sure where I intended to take her. I felt some time away from the resort might do her some good.

We didn't really do a whole lot of talking. There was something about her presence that remained a mystery. I was intrigued far more than I should have been, but I was going to go with my gut on this one.

Setting her cup down, she slid her chair back abruptly, taking my outstretched hand.

"Where to, Kekoa?"

I wasn't ready to let her in on that. I hadn't thought that far in advance. I was elated she agreed to go without putting up a fight, but I kept my cool, grabbing her hand and quickly turning to lead us towards the exit of the hotel restaurant.

I felt her slight tug and stopped to look back at her, ready to beg her to come with me if she tried to change her mind. But she just looked towards the elevators and said, "*Umm*... don't we need to put on some clothes first?"

"Nope."

"And I guess we're not going to be doing a whole lot of walking in these flip-flops then?"

I sighed and rolled my eyes dramatically in faux irritation before saying, "Woman, ain't nobody checking you out." *Better not be, I thought*. "You're fine."

She reluctantly tugged at her hair, which was growing into a bigger fiery ball with each passing second. A hint of worry flashed in her eyes.

I stopped and faced her a bit more seriously now. I cupped her chin, turning her face up to mine. "You're fine, Rhi. Beautiful."

Lips curling up into a lopsided smile, she dropped her hands to her side and nodded, "Let's go."

I'm not sure what she was feeling at that moment, but I could tell something or someone from her past was standing right there with Rhi at that moment. In that small flash of a decision to reclaim my hand and follow me to my truck, I recognized she had just won an internal battle. In that very moment, I knew exactly where we were going.

We rode in silence for the first 20 minutes of our trip. Rhi enjoyed the beautiful ocean views as she peered out the passenger window. We were heading north towards Ubud and the roads were higher, allowing her to take in the wide expanse of brilliant blue waters of the Indian Ocean and the coastline below. She peered past me through the driver's window at the starkly different scenery of rocky mountainside covered in lush greenery of the tropical forest. Either option was a beautiful spectacle, but she chose the ocean as her focus.

We drove further north until the ocean gave way to mountainous winding road. Noticing the change in landscape, Rhi asked, "You aren't trying to kidnap me, are you?" She half-joked, but she gave me a side-eye before continuing, "You said you wanted to show me something. I didn't think it was going to be out of town."

"Woman," I chuckled. "You cute and all, but there is no way I'd *willingly* kidnap your complaining ass."

"*Tuh*, I am not complaining. Just letting you know that I will crouching tiger, hidden dragon your ass before I let you."

"You are definitely showing your age, Rhi," I laughed, jerking away from the smack she was loading directed at my arm. We both burst out laughing.

It was good to see her smiling, something that didn't happen often in front of me before her injury. I caught glimpses of her joking with the other volunteers and being silly with the kids. I was happy to be getting some of this Rhi now.

"So, there is an old Balinese tale about an evil king, Myanmar," I said, trying to remember the exact name as Rhi stared at me with curious eyes. "No. Mayewa. King Mayewa! King Mayewa was really powerful, and it was widely known that he had some powers, though he wasn't a god. He was kind of feeling himself because of this, so he took it out on his subjects. He wouldn't let them worship or practice the Hindu religion."

"Yikes," she said, face scrunched into a comical pucker. "He sounds like a jerk."

"Big jerk," I nodded in agreement before continuing. "Soon the gods got wind of this, and they sent a real god, Indra, down to go straighten Mayewa out. So, Indra and his soldiers came, but Mayewa was crafty and used his power and evasion skills to lead Indra and his men on a cat and mouse chase all over the countryside. One day after several attempts and close encounters, the soldiers finally surrounded Mayewa. They didn't immediately attack and capture him because they wanted to rest and drink at the spring that was nearby. Well, Mayewa was slick. He crept down unnoticed and ended up poisoning the stream and many of the soldiers either died or became very ill. Now, Mayewa's cocky ass could have run and hidden, but he didn't which allowed Indra to catch up to him. Seeing all of his men dead or writhing in sickness, Indra struck the ground with his mighty staff and out flowed crystal-clear water. He told his sick men to drink and allowed the spring to run over the dead soldiers. As myth would have it, the god-touched water had magical healing powers which healed the sick and brought those that it touched back to life. After Indra's force was made whole again, they were able to finally defeat Mayewa."

I looked over at Rhi and found her so enthralled in the story that she didn't even notice we were stopping before the huge entrance to the Tirta Empul Temple. I nodded my head towards the entrance. Her eyes followed mine in wonder at the beautiful sight.

"This temple is told to be the location of the great battle between King Mayewa and the God Indra. It is known as the great battle of good versus evil."

Rhi looked at me in awe. "How do you know this tale?"

I looked away from her to mask the sudden emotion that was surely on my face. "My mother." I inhaled deeply. "This was one of her most favorite places in the world."

Rhi grabbed my hand and squeezed it gently. Taking a deep steadying breath, I said, "At least that's what my six-year-old self remembers."

"Six?" Rhi said, eyes full of questions.

Before she could ask anything, I bent and kissed her on the forehead and said, "Stay right here. I'll be right back."

I ran over to purchase two sarongs and sashes which were required to be worn by anyone seeking to enter the temple. I came back over to Rhi, handing her the more colorful of the two sarongs, explaining what they were for.

She looked at me teasingly as I explained to her how to wrap the skirt and the sash. "What?!" I asked in exasperation, failing to understand the humor in the situation.

She whistled and said, "*Mmm*, a big man in a skirt," and then whipped out her phone so damn fast to take a picture.

I sighed while trying to hide my smile. "*Ooh,* real funny, Rhi. You got me," I said in my best Drake impression, and then with more conceit, "Just so you know, I'm comfortable in my manhood. I look damn good in this skirt."

"Cocky motherfucker," she smirked. "You sound like the evil king from the tale."

"And for the record, it's a *kain kamben*. Now hush and bring your sexy, country ass on," I said close to her ear, chuckling at her slick joke but also trying not to touch her out of respect for where we were.

We entered the temple through the lush garden at its front. Rhi admired the brilliant tropical flowers and statues that lined the pathway to the temple gates. Before we entered, I looked down to admire Rhi. A calm suddenly came over her. I could tell she was deep in thought. The majesty of the temple could do that to you.

I came here many times after my mother's passing to bathe in the calming waters in hopes of restoring balance and peace within myself. I even brought Jada once, and her eight-year-old self expressed how calm she felt after entering the holy waters as well.

As we made it through the gates, Rhi gasped at the beauty of the courtyard to her right and the blue bathing pools to her left. Looking deeper into the courtyard, I watched her take in the 13 intricately carved purification spouts where devotees clasped their hands in prayer before ducking their heads one-by-one under the clear water pouring from the spouts into the larger pool of clear water.

She looked up at me in awe, "It's amazing, Kendrick."

I smiled at her before quietly guiding her to a wall lined with shoes. I looked at her looking at the shoes; I couldn't help but giggle when she watched me in horror take off my pair and add them to the line.

"I... *uh*, are we?"

I cut her off with a nod and waved over to a temple guide. I whispered to him in Balinese seeking permission to join the devotees in the purification bath. Once I explained my mother's devotion to Hinduism, he understood and granted permission. Typically, only pilgrims or Hindu and Buddhist devotees were allowed to enter the waters.

Again, looking down at Rhi, I said, "We are entering the waters. I think you will find that they are truly restorative and purifying." I continued more solemnly, "I've been able to find peace here." Another wave of emotion took over me, but I didn't try to mask it this time. "I don't claim to know your past experiences, but the look I see behind your eyes compelled me to bring you here." I grabbed her hand and led her down the few steps to the pool, instructing her to copy my movements and actions.

"Place your hands in prayer position like so."

She tentatively followed my lead.

"Then dip your head under each of the first eleven spouts."

"What about the last two?" she asked.

"Those are reserved for funerals and last rites."

She nodded in understanding.

"Under each spout, chant a small prayer about what you want to release and an equal prayer about what you want to manifest."

Again, she nodded in understanding, but this time her gaze was transfixed on the water like it had her under a spell. Under the water, I placed an encouraging hand on the small of her back to reassure her.

She followed me through the purification ritual from the first to the eleventh spout. I could tell she was moved by the experience. I wanted to wrap my arms around her but didn't. I remained silent, allowing her to feel her feelings. I led her to the place we left our shoes and other belongings, and then we headed back to the truck. Neither of us said a word.

Chapter 26 - Rhiyan

WE WERE HALFWAY BACK to the resort before Kendrick spoke. I knew he was driving in silence out of respect for me and the extreme emotions that must have been pervading my body.

I felt different after ducking my head under that first spout. By the time I made it to the sixth spout, tears were streaming down my face, hidden only by the water that ran in rivulets from my dripping coils. By the time I made it to my final prayer under the last spout, the tears were gone, and I felt a power within that I hadn't felt since before my divorce—since before Kyle introduced himself to me as the thing he really was. A liar and a cheat.

Under that last spout, I realized I'd been praying the whole time for forgiveness. Not for myself, but for the power to forgive him for making me become the Rhi that had been hiding in despair and self-pity and hurt over the last year. I felt the power running through my veins and it humbled me.

When we got back to the truck to leave, I grabbed Kendrick's hand but couldn't find any words. He understood my need for his comfort. It was in that moment I also knew that what I'd prayed to manifest was a me who could show up authentically. The me who knew love would come again, but also the me who would not chase it under any circumstances. In the moment of that realization, Kendrick whispered, "I know, sweetheart. I felt it, too."

Our silence continued even after we made it back to the resort. Kendrick led me through the lobby to the elevators and instead of pushing the button to my floor, he inserted his key card, and we rode to the top of the building to his room.

The elevator opened to the large opulent living room. I didn't pay much attention to the marble floors earlier this morning when we came for Kendrick's swim trunks. Now, I stared in wonder at the gold and beige veining that curled like tendrils of smoke across the entire expanse of the suite.

I felt Kendrick walk up behind me and wrap his large arms around my torso. I leaned back into him for a minute just to enjoy the cocoon of safety his arms provided. The sensation of his hard arms wrapped around my body caused a dam within me to break.

My desire for this man flowed through like rushing water. My skin ached to feel his lips and hands. He smelled of warm amber; it pervaded my senses, enveloping me with his scent. I turned into his embrace, raising on my toes to reach my arms around his neck and pulling him down so that our lips crashed into each other. The kiss was soft at first but grew more frenzied. I felt reborn.

Tension built from a small flicker to a burning flame in that very instance. All of the need I felt this morning when I almost pulled my swim bottom to the side came rushing back but on ten. Kendrick groaned as my passion took him by surprise, too. It was consuming.

"Where's the bathroom?" I asked after pulling away from him suddenly. He pointed but my lips were back on his before he could utter a word. I led him backwards in the direction that he pointed, not wanting to be out of his grasp for even a second.

My shaking hands fumbled with the drawstring of his still damp shorts, and I groaned in frustration beneath his lips. "Let me help," Kendrick hissed, breaking our kiss briefly, swiping my hands away to untie the string. He then gathered the fabric of my swimsuit cover up, yanking the material over my head in one fluid motion. His trunks dropped between us as he leaned back in to plant hot kisses along my neck.

"I want to taste all of you," he muttered as he hooked an index finger under each of the thin straps of the swimsuit. After moments of stripping, snatching, tasting, and sighing in a room where time stood still, we were both naked, skin-to-skin, suddenly in the entrance of the bathroom. *When did we get here? How?*

He pressed his forehead to mine with his eyes closed as if that gesture would slow the beating of his heart. I wasn't sure if it was his or mine or both of ours in tandem beating to the same rhythm. He opened his eyes. There was a raging battle within them as he looked down at me, trying to maintain his composure. I could tell he was at his limit and was ready to slam into me but was fighting heaven and earth to follow my lead.

I turned my attention to the mirror and could see the silhouettes of our bodies. I'd normally never stare at my own naked form in the mirror. This time, I was mesmerized at the erotic sight of our naked forms. His eyes were on me in that mirror, too. My eyes moved down the mirrored version of his chest to the protruding dick that stood massively between us, pressing into the softness of my bellybutton.

"Kendrick," I sighed.

"Yes, baby," he mumbled as his lips wrapped around the peak of one erect nipple.

"Turn the shower on."

Not letting me go or releasing my nipple, he backed me into the bathroom and reached blindly to turn on the luxurious shower-head.

We continued kissing until we both felt the steam of the hot water permeate the bathroom. He picked me up, wrapping my legs around his waist again. This man was driving me wild with that shit; it turned my ass on even more knowing he was powerful enough to handle me like he wanted to. The hot water washed over us as a wave of heat washed over me.

He grabbed the shower gel and rubbed it over my body, focusing gently on my swollen clit and between my legs. He gently stroked as I closed my eyes and moaned. I grabbed the bottle and returned the favor. First lathering his chest then moving down his hard abs and that sexy-ass cutline that led to the thick, dark silky hairs surrounding his long shaft that I couldn't wait to wrap my mouth around. We stroked each other to a frenzy.

"*Ahh*," Kendrick groaned deliciously. "Vixen," he warned, "You're going to make me... *ahh*." The steady beat of the shower drowned out his words.

I slowed my stroke to a torturous rhythm, trying my best to ring out his happy ending. The nasty things that came from my mouth sounded far away as if spoken by someone else. I was shocked at the audacity of my own words. Yet the louder he groaned; the more daring were the words I uttered. He turned my ass around, placing both hands on the shower wall, giving me an anchor before he slammed full force into me.

"*Ahh*, Kendrick. *Yesss*," I moaned as he slowed his pace but stroked me harder and deeper. I felt the fullness of his long dick inside me. He filled me up. I didn't want him to cum like that so I changed up our position again, dropping to my knees, allowing him to slip out of me and turned to come face-to-face with that beautiful monster.

I gave him no mercy as I wrapped both hands around the base of his throbbing dick and popped the head right into my hungry-ass mouth. I sucked the head while simultaneously looking deep into his eyes, not giving a damn that the water from the shower was pouring down on us. I refused to break eye contact as I slid him in a little further, inch-by-inch while twisting my hands around the base in a pepper-grinding motion.

"*Ahhh*," he moaned louder, this time putting his hands on the shower wall and the glass to keep his balance. He threw his head back as the waves of his release took over. I sucked harder, twisting my hands faster, trying to get him there. I needed him to cum almost as bad as he wanted to. And then... it happened. Hot spurts of sweet honey in my mouth.

His ejaculation was powerful, almost causing me to choke. I held it together, and that just made my mouth wetter. I continued to lick and suck. His body convulsed. He groaned as his knees went weak. "*Got damn*, Vixen." He almost lost his balance.

It was empowering to almost bring this hulking specimen of a man to his knees, but my power was short-lived as he pulled me up to meet his chest, this time slamming his lips into mine. One arm wrapped around my waist as he turned the shower off with the other hand.

He half-dragged, half-pushed me onto the bed, tossing me like a rag doll to its center. He grabbed my ankles and yanked them apart just before planting his mouth on my pussy. I fucking lost it.

What was I supposed to do other than ride the wave? I moaned and rocked my hips into his face. Reckless abandon as I moaned, "Yes, baby... like that. *Please...*"

This man was making a habit of making me beg and he did not disappoint. He ate my pussy like it was the only meal he'd had all day. He licked and explored my entire essence, using his face, fingers and that magical tongue.

My body shook uncontrollably. The orgasm snuck up on me. I was so into the moment that I didn't even feel the tightening of my pelvic floor until it was too late. My whole musculo-skeleton must have locked up because I was frozen and powerless to fight the wave of the orgasm ripping through my body. By the time my legs were limp enough to unwrap from around Kendrick's neck, I was sobbing uncontrollably.

The weight of his body crushed the bed as he climbed to its center, pulling me on top of him for a hug. Tears continued to spring from my eyes as I unloaded all the emotions that overcame me today. I told him about my prayers, I told him about the divorce, I told him about fucking up at work. I told this man everything. And just like his chest soaked up my tears, he soaked up my pain and let me cry until I was spent.

Chapter 27 - Kendrick

Waking up to Rhi's beautiful face was quickly becoming a favorite pastime. Her hair haloed around her head, giving her an angelic peaceful essence, which was a far cry from the emotionally charged night we had. She unexpectedly opened up to me.

In the past, a woman's tears were usually a cue that it was time to call it quits. Leave scene. Exit now. With Rhi, it was different. I was different. We were different. As her delicate tears fell, the only urge I felt was to wipe them away and hug her tighter, to shield her from the pain of her past and fear of the future.

I had a newfound respect for her and a much deeper understanding of why she had been cold to me in the beginning. Her words from last night replayed as I reached to rub her cheek with the back of my hand.

"The bastard cheated with our neighbor of *all* people. It broke my heart," she sobbed onto my chest. "I tried to be perfect for him.

Perfect wife, perfect lover. I wanted to be the perfect mother, but it wasn't in the cards."

Damn, I thought, but said nothing. I just rubbed her back so she could get it out.

"I had no right to take that out on you, Kendrick," she continued.

"*Shhh*. I know," I consoled. "Just let it out, baby."

After she told me about the divorce and all the things she dealt with, I finally understood all the eyerolls, the side-eyes, and contemptuous stares. I admired the courage it must have taken to let her guard down. My chest tightened from the feeling of connectedness I felt with her. It felt right. Meant to be. Like we had known each other all along. I felt like her protector.

We laughed uncontrollably—she through muffled sniffles and I through loud sporadic grunts—when she explained how her ex used to wear his shades at night all the time. He thought he looked cool. She thought it made him look like a pompous ass. It explained why me wearing Ray Bans on the night of our first encounter turned out to be a massive trigger for her.

I chuckled and held her tighter as I explained that I had just gotten off the long flight from Hawaii to Bali, and after seeing my own bloodshot eyes in the very same mirror she was checking herself out in before colliding with the porter, I decided I would rather look like a fool wearing shades at night than walk around with red-rimmed, bloodshot eyes. That made her laugh again through the tears I was kissing away.

We lounged on the bed, enjoying the comfortable silence. And it occurred to me that I would indeed spend a lifetime trying to erase those triggers and their consequential pain. The thought surprised me as much today as the similar thought surprised me last night when she cried in my arms. I pondered it for a moment, coming to terms with its truth. It had only been a small while, but I really did care deeply for this woman. I wanted to share my dreams, my life with her. *When you know, you know.*

Given the gravity of our relationship, I also knew I would soon have to tell her about Jada. Admittedly, I was a bit nervous about that. I never really got close to anyone enough to go about telling them much about my personal life. Where would I even start? "Hi, I'm Kendrick and I'm a single father," sounded like something you'd hear in a Hallmark movie when the small-town, widowed father finally decides to start dating again.

And how would I tell her about my strange relationship with Jade? I didn't particularly care to discuss Jade with anyone, but Rhi needed to know about Jade's issues and her popping in and out of our lives. Well, not my life. I stopped that years ago. I was old enough to know most women have a low tolerance for that shit. *Hell, I'm jumping the gun. What if she doesn't even want me that way?*

True, we had amazing sex, and I enjoyed spending time holed up in her company. I'd fallen, but had she? There was only one way to find out. And that was by talking to her.

I laid there for a little while longer, thinking through how I'd bring up the conversation and decided it would be best to do it outside of the bedroom. *Dinner.* Nice, quiet candle-lit dinner for two.

I was excited about the prospect of seeing where Rhi and I could take this thing we had together. We did live on opposite ends of the country, maybe this was a nonstarter. My mind was see-sawing up and down between happiness at the potential of becoming serious with Rhi and the apprehension that she may not feel the same way. It was a conversation to be had, but not today. Today, she needed to smile, and I had just the thing to get her to do that.

By the time Sleeping Beauty had awakened, I'd slipped out of bed and used the spare key provided by the hotel front desk on the day of the quake to go get some of Rhi's things from her room, namely her hair-care products. Her hair was completely soaked yesterday at the temple and again as we made love in the shower. After years of learning how to take care of Jada's curly hair, I knew Rhi was going to have a time with her matted cloud of coils.

I also took the liberty of going through her closet to grab another swimsuit, a pair of cutoff jean shorts, and a pair of her flip-flops. I knew I was taking a risk here because what woman wants a man rummaging through her private things? Yet, I didn't feel like I was invading her personal space. And that in itself was a milestone in my relationship with her. I was no longer a stranger in the setting of her life.

Finally, I stopped at the on-site coffee shop to grab two lattes. She was going to need it after crying half the night. She was stirring out of sleep as I came back into the bedroom.

"Get up, sleepyhead," I coaxed her, standing at her side of the bed and holding the coffee out to her.

"God bless you," she said, arm still thrown across her face to ward off the light streaming through the partially opened blinds. The smooth aroma of the coffee and salted caramel flavor wafted from the cup and appeared to beckon her eyes open. "Do you always know what to do and say, Mr. Kekoa?" she asked, finally sitting up.

"Well, you know, I *am* the man," I replied all cocky and arrogant before I had to side-step the pillow she flung in my direction. "Hey, now! No need for violence," I chided her. "Plus, you're going to need all your strength to tackle that bird's nest on your head."

The look of mortification on her face was priceless as she damn near dropped her coffee in her haste to conceal her messy hair. "*Ugh*," she groaned. "It's going to take four hands and two Denman brushes to get my hair together!"

"And you are still the most beautiful lady in this whole resort,"
I said as I sat at her side and wrapped an arm around the small of
her waist, pulling her closer. "I passed by your room to get some of
your things," I peppered her with kisses before leaning forward to
grab the beach bag between my feet. "Now, hurry with that coffee
and go get dressed!"

Chapter 28 – Kendrick

AN HOUR LATER, Rhi and I were standing at the concierge's desk in the lobby of the resort, waiting for them to bring around two scooters that I reserved while waiting for our coffee earlier. They'd handed over our helmets, and Rhi was strapping hers on with a childlike excitement as I let her in on what we had in store for the day.

Before the concierge walked away to get the scooters ready, Rhi yelled after him, "Can I get a purple one?"

He turned around and bowed at her, "Yes, ma'am. As you wish. And for the gentleman?"

"I'll have something a little less girly and that has been lifted," I said.

The concierge looked at my broad frame and long legs and nodded in complete understanding. "Coming right up," he said with flourish and hurried away.

"Kendrick, you have to get a picture of me on my scooter! No one is going to believe I did this without proof." The coffee must have had her wired or the prospect of zipping through these Bali streets was such a thrill to her that I forgot how melancholic she was the night before; it seemed like a lifetime ago. *So far so good on 'Mission Make Rhi Smile Today'.*

Moments later, we were off. Surprisingly, she caught on pretty fast and was stealthily riding the two-wheeled machine. Before long, she was zipping past me; each time looking back to challenge me to keep up. We rode like this for a while until I yelled over to get her attention, "Hey, let me take the lead. I have a surprise for you."

Twenty minutes later, we pulled into the parking lot overlooking Pantai Pandawa, one of the public beaches mostly frequented by the locals. The parking lot flanked a colorful boardwalk that had shops and eateries to buy gifts, various sundries such as suntan lotion, sarongs, or swimsuits, and of course, food and beverages for the beachgoers who worked up an appetite.

As soon as we dismounted and stowed our helmets, Rhi grabbed her beach bag and my hand and dragged me to one of the shops that had colorful sarongs and beach hats on display. She grabbed one of the big floppy hats and paired it with a large pair of sunglasses.

"How do I look?" she asked striking a sexy pose, looking back at me over her lifted, copper-dipped shoulder.

I inched closer and pulled her back into my chest, planting a kiss on her upturned lips while signaling to the young lady behind the register that we'd take both. I released my grip on her and handed over enough rupia to pay for the items and leave a sizable tip.

"Wait," Rhi implored, fingering a wooden-carved pair of large earrings. "These too, please," she said, handing them over to cashier then reaching into her bag to pull out her rupia.

I stopped her hand before she could hand over any money, "Put that back, Rhi." I gave her a pat on the behind and then playfully nipped the same shoulder she raised earlier. "Whatever the lady wants today, the lady shall get."

This time, she turned in my arms, draping the length of hers over my shoulders. "Is that so?" she asked seductively.

"Anything you want, Rhi," I tilted my head down placing my forehead on hers. "Your wish is my command."

She tilted her head back, placing her index finger to her cheek as if in deep thought. "Okay. I want..." she drew out the words, making me wait for her wish, "to ride on that boat over there," she finally said, pointing to the sleek white sailboat that bobbed out in the brilliant blaze of sunshine and sparkling water.

The shop keeper handed me a receipt along with the bag of items we purchased, and we made our way down to the beach and rented a boat.

"Do you know what you are doing, Kendrick?" Rhi asked when she realized that the boat didn't come with a captain to drive it.

I chuckled as the boat engine roared to life as I stood at its helm and skillfully pulled us out into the Indian Ocean. "There is not much I cannot do on the water, Vixen." I looked back at her and said, "Put on your seatbelt and relax. I got this."

I was in my element. I often rented a boat to take Jada and Ona out on the water back home. I had been wanting to buy a sailboat for years now, just never got the time.

The boat zipped through the blue waters like a hot knife through butter. I enjoyed watching Rhi look out at the rushing waves as we passed through them. Her smile never wavered as she held her new hat down on her head to keep the wind from carrying it away as we raced out deeper in the blue waters. When the shoreline was barely visible, I slowed and cut the engine's power.

I locked the steering wheel as I walked back to where Rhi was sitting. She stood slowly, testing out her sea legs as I pulled her into another embrace to steady her. "Come up to the front with me," I said, then reached into one of the compartments on the other side of the seating area, pulling out a thin blanket and a picnic basket that came with the rental. The compartment was refrigerated to keep the grapes, cheese, meats, and wine that were in the basket cold.

"How did you know that was in there?" Rhi asked, pleasantly surprised.

"I selected the honeymoon package along with the boat rental," I said, eyeing her to see if that made her uncomfortable in any way. I wasn't trying to push anything on her, I just wanted the food and wine so we could stay out on the water longer.

"I am convinced, that there is nothing you don't think about," she shook her head in wonder as we made our way up to the nose of the boat to spread out the blanket to lounge and explored the contents of the basket.

She fished out two small plates and filled them with food for the both of us, while I found the corkscrew for the wine bottle and two wine glasses. I filled them to the top, handing her one as I tasted mine.

She, in turn, placed a large, green grape into my mouth. She then pulled her fingers from my lips to replace them with her lips and bit half of the grape that was settled between my teeth, allowing the sweet juiciness to run down our chins. I pulled her in closer, almost making her spill her wine to explore her mouth better with my tongue.

I tasted the sweetness of the grapes and the tartness of the wine on her tongue as I deepened the kiss. She pulled away and playfully swiped my lips with her tongue to say, "This is amazing,

Kendrick," before turning to settle into the crook of my arm and lifting the wine glass to her lips.

We sat like that for a while, enjoying the wine and taking turns feeding each other off our respective plates. We could see other boats dotting the water in the distance, but none came close to us. We were in our own private slice of the Bali blue water. Heaven.

After we finished eating, Rhi decided to take off the cutoffs she'd worn over her swimsuit so she could soak in some of the sun's rays and catch a tan. I watched her lie down and prop herself on her elbows, legs stretched out in front of her. I studied her studying the ocean.

Her hair was pulled back into an elegant bun at the nape of her neck and shoulders. The sun glistened off the exposed parts of her breasts and off the tops of her thighs. Her smooth skin shone like molten caramel under the brilliance of the midday sun, beckoning me. I crawled to her.

I kissed the same shoulder that I nipped earlier. This time, I allowed the wetness of my tongue to glide over her shoulder then down her collarbone to the cleft between her breasts. *"Mmm,"* she moaned as I sank my lips around one nipple and then the other that sprang to life under the confines of her swimsuit. I made no move to free her breasts. I sucked them through the fabric, allowing the friction and the wetness of my mouth to create new sensations.

I abandoned her breasts and planted kisses down her stomach to the top of the V between her thighs. She took in an involuntary hiss between her lips in anticipation, grabbed the sides of my head to guide me to her spot. I gently moved past her covered pussy to plant wet kisses down the tops of her thighs and licked down and behind each of her knees, causing her hips to begin wriggling against the smooth carbon fiber of the boat's hood.

I licked and nibbled my way back up to her mound and kissed around it as I searched for my half empty wine glass. I nudged her legs further apart as I settled between them on my knees. I tipped the wine glass to my lips as I looked down at her. Her eyes locked on mine, a glaze of passion and lust in them. I swallowed the wine then bent at the waist, hovering my mouth just over the apex of her thighs, never taking my eyes off hers.

"Do you want me to taste you, Rhi?" I questioned; voice thick, mirroring the lust in her eyes.

She closed her eyes; her hips rose towards me as she uttered a moan dripping, "Yes, Kendrick. Please."

She reached her hands down attempting to move her bikini bottoms to the side so I could get to her swollen, juicy pleasure beneath, but I swatted her hands away. Again, she moaned, "Please, Kendrick. I need you. Need to feel you." Her words trailing off as another moan involuntarily escaped her lips and I licked her through the fabric of the bikini.

At this point she was almost in a frenzy, biting down on her bottom lip to keep from falling apart. It was then that I splashed some of the cool wine from my glass between her legs then promptly bent down to suck the wine and her clit through her bikini.

When I slid her bottoms to the side to finally taste and lick her swollen wetness, her hands cupped the nape of my neck and held me tightly in place. I reveled in the taste of her. I love the smell and feel of her shaved pussy against my tongue and nose. I wanted more and reached under her to grasp the stretchy fabric, ripping the briefs down and over the swell of her hips to her ankles. She freed one of them as I pushed her knees apart and buried my face again between her knees.

Moments later she came. I wasted no time, sinking inside her to find my own release.

Chapter 29 - Rhiyan

I T FELT GOOD BEING back at the center with the kids. Not as good as it felt in Kendrick's big bed wrapped in his massive, yet surprisingly gentle arms. It certainly didn't feel as good as our encounter on the boat in broad daylight. But I missed the little rug rats at the center and was glad to be back. I especially missed Naijah and couldn't wait to see what new dance routine she mastered for Tik Tok in the three days I'd been out.

I arrived at the center just after 8 a.m. to get caught up and see what I missed out on in my absence. I passed Dominic's class on the way to mine, stopping in his doorway to quickly say hi because I could tell he was engrossed in his class prep and lesson planning.

At first, he absently threw up a hand to return a hello, but his intended quick glance became a full-on double take before his face split into a huge smile. "Hi beautiful. You're back!" he said in a long, drawn-out tone as he gave me his full attention. "Gro gave us the message that you were resting and were doing fine so we didn't bother you. How is that head of yours?"

"Oh, I'm fine," I said, leaning against the door jam and crossing my arms. "Just a small cut and a bruise that you can't even see." I pressed my hand to the bun at the crown of my head. "All of this hair must have cushioned the blow," I shrugged, hoping to erase the genuine look of concern on his face. It must have worked because his gaze turned from concern to nosy suspicion.

He moved a bit closer to the doorway where I stood, pausing at arm's length away and tilting his head. He peered at me through narrowed eyes while tapping the index finger of his right hand softly against his lips as he continued his deep perusal of me. My face scrunched under his scrutiny before he finally spoke.

"You look positively radiant, *ma cherie*." His smile deepened as he slowly turned back toward the board he'd been studying so intently when I first walked in and began slowly walking back towards it. I felt like he was dismissing me so I started backing out the door.

"You have a freshly fucked look about you," he said nonchalantly before I could make it out the door.

My hand flew up to cover the involuntary gasp that escaped my lips. *Busted.*

I fixed my face in the best surprised look possible, hoping to disqualify his comment by doing so. "Hush, Dominic," I reprimanded him and hurried out of his class.

"You didn't deny it though! Love you, Rhi!" His screams chased me down the hallway. More laughter. "Glad you're back."

As I suspected, Jen and Francis were both in one of the classrooms at the end of the hall huddled in hushed conversation at one of the kid-sized tables in the back of the room. I could tell they were gossiping from the sneaky looks and hushed laughs they shared.

"What are you ladies gossiping about?" I asked, announcing my presence in the room.

Jen squealed as she jumped up arms wide for an embrace. "I'm so happy you're okay!" she gushed, holding me out at arm's length to look me over.

"You're alive and still cute," Francis added. "I'm so glad you weren't seriously injured. I heard the area of the building you were in sustained the only real damage." She too gave me a similar up and down look as Dominic had given me minutes before. "You look... *um,* well rested," she continued as if something were different about me that she couldn't quite put her finger on. Letting the notion go, she also wrapped me in a quick hug. It was then that it hit me, Jeff wasn't in his class.

"Where's Jeff?" I asked.

More sneaky looks were exchanged between the two confirming he was the topic of their conversation. I looked back and forth between Jen and Francis. "Spit it out," I said, arms crossed and eyes narrowed.

They both burst out into giggles. It was Jen who spoke first. "He'll beeee" she stretched out the 'be', "a little late today." She then pointed her finger in the face of a blushing Francis before continuing, "Because someone fucked his brains out last night."

"Wait. What?" I almost choked, rounding on Francis. "When did this happen?" It was amazing how much could change in a mere three days. I said as much. "I leave here for three days, and all hell breaks loose," I said in jest as Francis finally found her voice. She pressed her hand to her now red cheeks, slightly embarrassed. She took a deep steadying breath and groaned before spilling all the tea.

"Well, he'd been flirting with me the night we all went out to see the fire dance."

"You mean when you disappeared?" I asked Francis while directing my scrunched brow at Jen. "I thought you said she went back to her room?"

Jen looked guilty at getting caught in her little white lie before speaking, "Well, she did..."

Francis cut her off, "I did go to my room. Just not alone."

"I see," I said, turning my full attention back to Francis. "Continue," I urged, narrowing my eyes at her but not quite able to keep the corners of my lips from contorting at the corners into a conspiratorial smile. I noticed how they used to flirt with each other, but I surely was interested in hearing how this had progressed to her 'fucking his brains out' as Jen so eloquently put it.

"Jen and I ran into him and Dominic after we all left the beach. We were all tipsy and that southern American boy charm got to me," she whined in her sing-song Brazilian accent.

"I knew there was something between the two of you!" I exclaimed in an excited whisper. "Guess you better be ready to take care of his class and your own today."

She threw her head back in exasperation, face all balled up as she damn near stumped like a petulant child. "I know right! Fuck!" Jen and I both burst out laughing as we all disbursed to go to greet the vans of children that arrived.

The day went by quickly, and just like I knew she would, Naijah showed me her new dance moves. Kendrick had told me she didn't have a single scratch on her from the hospital, and Gro confirmed that when he stopped by to check up on me at my hotel. I was so glad to lay eyes on her and see for myself that she was okay. She'd been through a rough ordeal but seemed to be just fine.

Apparently, she formed a little dance crew with the other girls her age and had perfected the moves to a new Tik Tok challenge. They all knew the moves and took turns showing me their own rendition of the dance. I was here for it, cheering them on at recess like I was the team mom.

Today was a short day, so the kids were gone, and I was in class preparing for the next day when I felt someone come up behind me. Before I could turn to check who it was, strong arms circled around my waist, pulling me backwards into the hard wall of his chest. "*Mmm*," I moaned, knowing exactly who it was by the electricity between us that made the tiny hairs at the back of my neck stand.

He ran his lips over the tiny pulse in the small space just above where my neck and shoulder met, then whispered in my ear. "Will you do the honor of going to dinner with me this evening, Ms. Carson?"

My knees literally went weak as the softness of his words oozed like warm honey across my eardrum. His warm lips followed suit across my lobe as he nibbled it softly with his teeth before sucking it between his warm lips. I melted. Then I turned in his arms, breaking the contact of his lips to look up into his eyes, rising on my toes to wrap my arms around his neck. "Of course, I will, Mr. Kekoa. What are you doing here?" I purred languidly as I relaxed into his arms, forgetting we were in the middle of my classroom.

"Trying to ask you to dinner, ma'am," he said, planting a kiss on my lips.

"What do you have in mind?" I asked, looking down suggestively where our bodies were pressed tightly together at the hips. He chuckled, gently grabbing my chin to guide my eyes back up to his.

"Absolutely, I want to taste *that,*" he glanced down ever so slightly at my kitty cat, "But that's desert," he raised his eyebrows, meeting his forehead to mine. "I was thinking maybe we could actually eat food and talk outside of the bedroom.

"Oh," I said, eyes betraying brief disappointment. "Good idea. We've done a lot more touching and groping than talking, huh?" I asked, blushing at the thought of all the grown-folk things we'd been doing over the last few days.

He pinched his chin and tilted his head as if to recall what we'd been doing before nodding his head quickly up and down. "Yeah. Lots of touching, moaning, kissing, licking," he paused to give me another peck on the lips. "How about an actual date? Dinner, wine, conversation. We can get dressed up in our finest beach resort wear, and I can meet you at your room at 7 p.m. for a quick stroll down to the resort restaurant." He smiled, lifting his brow in question to see what I thought.

It really was a good idea, to get a chance to talk and get to know each other outside of the confines of my bed or his. Plus, I know we hadn't known each other that long, but the tides had turned quickly on us, and I wanted to talk to him about my time in Bali coming to an end in just shy of a week. Maybe I was being foolish and naïve, but I wanted to get a sense of 'where do we go from here?'

"I will be ready promptly at 7 p.m."

With that, he took my hand and stepped back before leaning in to kiss it in a gentlemanly bow. He walked towards the door and said, "I'll see you later, Ms. Carson."

I stared after him with a lusty, wistful smile on my face, glad no one had seen our exchange. I just wanted to savor our little secret and not have to explain to Jen, Francis, or that damn spidey-sense having Dominic. I could tell that his ass knew what was up between Kendrick and I from our exchange in his classroom this morning. Jeff was the only one who seemed to be minding his business today. I'd seen him sneak in a couple of hours ago, just after lunch.

Chapter 30 – Kendrick

I WAS EXCITED, YET still nervous about my date with Rhi tonight. I had a lot to get done before heading back to the resort to get ready. After leaving the school, I made my way to Micah to see how progress on the road construction was going because I needed to provide a status update to Ketut.

I pulled up to the worksite and patiently waited to get Micah's attention. He was doing quality control on the paving of a stretch of road just on the outskirts of the city center. I could hear him calling out in satisfaction of the work that the road crew was doing before I finally caught his attention and waved him over.

Work was progressing better than I could have hoped, and we were nearly done with our assignment here. The minister had made good on his promise that the equipment would be in place for the road crews, construction teams, electrical and plumbing teams. That was massively helpful. When it came down to it, my team and I were here mostly in a consulting, planning, and evaluation capacity. The crews were good at what they did, and we were slightly ahead of schedule.

"Yo!" I yelled over the loud noise of the paver. "Looks like you are wrapping up over here."

"You damn right, brah. These teams are the truth. A few more feet of paving and we're calling it a day on this side." As he spoke, he was focused on removing the huge orange Road Work sign. It was weighted at the end with a concrete footing so as not to fall over no matter how hard the crosswinds blew. I rushed over to help him lift it into the back of one of the work trucks.

After we finished wrestling with the heavy sign, he finally gave me his undivided attention.

"You finally decide to grace us with your presence, eh?" Micah asked with a playful grin on his face. "How is the Ice Queen doing? Wait, is she still the Ice Queen or did you finally warm her up?" He chuckled side stepping the daggers my eyes threw at him.

"Mind your business, man," I said, not giving anything away.

"Just kidding, brah," he chuckled as he turned back to grab and stack more of the orange cones into the back of the work truck.

Changing the subject away from Rhi, I said, "Looks like we only have about a week's worth of work remaining here. Go ahead and finish up and move the crew up North to complete the roads leading up to the mountain passes on the west side of the island. The east is done, right?"

"Yep, you know we don't play. We should be able to knock out the west side in two days," Micah said as cock-sure as the man-bun on top of his head.

"Sweet. I need to go check in with the minister and let him know the progress. Hit me on the walkie if you need me," I said, dapping Micah up.

I jumped in my truck and headed over to Ketut's office. The roads were looking damn good. We'd made sure to influence the planning to include greening the highways and created a new system of roads that could circumvent future erosion to withstand the toughest of earthquakes.

Twenty minutes later, I was seated inside the minister's office waiting on him to finish up a call. When done, he came around the desk bear hugging me and pounding my back.

"Kendrick, I hear everything is going smoothly with the reconstruction." He held me out at arm's length, gracing me with a beaming ear-to-ear smile as was his customary sunny disposition. "Give me an update, won't you," he said, releasing me and ambling back around to his seat behind the desk.

I sat in one of the leather chairs in front and proceeded to give him a full update on all the efforts to get Bali back into full swing. "The roadwork will be completed within the week, and we hope to have full internet and phone service across Bali and Lombok back up within two weeks. My crew will be packing to leave as soon as that is completed.

"As always, Kekoa's expertise has rebuilt Bali to be bigger, stronger, and better than we've ever been to withstand these earthquakes that are all too familiar in the region," he sat forward, pinning me with a look of satisfaction as he continued. "For that, we will be releasing a series of articles and press releases highlighting the contributions that you and your company have made to Bali's resiliency and its future sustainability against natural disasters."

He pulled in his press secretary to take notes in preparation for the first article that would highlight Kekoa's use of recycled concrete from all the rubble mixed with our patented formula using volcanic rock and microalgae to reduce debris in the offshore landfills. The article was going to shake up the construction industry, placing Kekoa Industries as a firm leader in sustainable construction.

He continued to lay out the concept for two additional articles that would be released in order one week after the other with the last one detailing the work we'd put into making safer roads and safer buildings and how those two efforts would bolster Bali's already thriving tourist economy.

"Minister, I appreciate the writeups about Kekoa, but want you to know that this is what we do. With or without the kudos. We came because you called. You are family. Bali is just as much my home as Hawaii."

"And that is even more of a reason you should be recognized," Ketut said, standing and reaching his hand out to shake mine over the desk. I grabbed his and shook it firmly in preparation to leave.

We both turned in surprise as his office door flew open and his secretary rushed in holding a satellite phone outstretched to me. Concern was etched on her face as she announced, "Mr. Kekoa, there's been an emergency."

I took the phone and lifted it to my ear, looking at Ketut in confusion. "Hello?"

The phone fell from my hand as I bolted towards the door, calling over my shoulder to Ketut, "TiTi Ona had a heart attack!"

I hightailed it to the resort to grab my things before jetting to the airport.

Chapter 31 - Rhiyan

SEVEN O'CLOCK AND NO Kendrick. By 7:30, I figured maybe I had the instructions wrong. Instead of him meeting me at my hotel room, maybe I was supposed to meet him in the lobby or at the restaurant.

I grabbed my room key and headed down. He was not in the lobby and the maitre'd at the restaurant had the reservation for our table for two, but Kendrick wasn't in the restaurant. I went to the concierge's desk and had them call up to his room. I knew I wouldn't be able to access his penthouse suite without an access card for the elevator. No answer in his room.

It wasn't until the next morning when I awoke and still hadn't heard from him that I began to worry. Another day went by without any word from him, and my anxiety was turning into anger.

It had been three days and I had not seen nor heard from Kendrick. I couldn't help but think this man had ghosted me. This island wasn't that big, and I'd seen some of his men about, so I knew his company was still here. On the fourth day, I saw Micah at one of the renovated buildings across from the school. Throwing caution to the wind, I walked across the street to just straight up ask him where his boss was. "Hey there," I said hesitantly. "Have you by chance seen Kendrick?"

He looked at me a bit hesitantly as if not quite sure how much he was at liberty to say. I stuttered, nervously adding, "There is something I wanted him to take a look at in the school." *Lies.* I didn't want him thinking I was pressed.

"Oh," he said, as if suddenly remembering. "Kendrick had to go back to the States. He had a family emergency with his kid."

His kid...? This man had a kid that he never mentioned?

"Family emergency, *huh*?" I asked through the fake-ass smile pasted on my face. "*Uh*, ok." I wasn't doing a good job at hiding my confusion and utter anger at this point. I wanted to press Micah for more information but didn't want to run the risk of looking like an even bigger fool to believe Kendrick and I were anything... *had* anything more than great sex. I started walking back across the street throwing my hand up over my shoulder with a curt, "Thanks, Micah."

He yelled behind me, "Is everything okay at the school? Anything I can chec-"

I cut him off before he could finish, tossing a terse, "Nope," over my shoulder. "Everything is fine. It will be just *fine*."

I needed to get away before I gave away my hurt and disappointment in Kendrick to his friend. I sucked it up, took a deep breath, and entered the school. I felt the hot tears starting to pool but refused to let them drop. Opting to give myself the biggest pep talk of my life, channeling every ounce of Jai I could muster.

Did you find your crown, bitch? Check.

Did you help them kids? Check.

Did you make new friends? Check.

Did you bounce on some Asian dick? Well, *umm...* yes and no. It wasn't Asian but half-Hawaiian and half-black. And it was *tantric*. Check, *checkity*, check, check, check.

Welp sounds like you're winning. Take your ass on home.

Chapter 32 - Rhiyan

IT WAS KIND OF bittersweet to be back home in Atlanta. It was a fact that I'd trade the lush tropics and beautiful beaches of Bali for the dense traffic, skyscrapers, and tree-lined streets of the A. The one thing that both places had in common was this damn humidity and heat. It shocked but didn't surprise me that the temps were still in the 90s in mid-September in Atlanta.

I'd been home for just over a week and had only talked to Jai'Elle once when my flight landed. It was high time for us to get together and catch up. We decided to meet for early dinner and drinks at one of our favorite restaurants on the westside of the city.

I blasted the speakers in my Audi SUV as I drove while seat-dancing, pointing at myself in the rear-view mirror as I fake lip-synched the lyrics to a catchy tune I hadn't heard before. It was something about *F-boys messing it up for real men* and was a whole vibe that had me feeling good and acting silly. I missed rolling through the city with my music loud. I missed having impromptu concerts with myself—as the entertainer and the audience—while performing to the rearview mirror.

It was amazing how much had changed for the better in the last couple of months. The drive from my office to my home prior to my trip to Bali had felt like walking the green mile. But now, it was like the city was painted in vibrant, living color; and I loved it here. I wanted to get out and do stuff, and the drive to the restaurant felt exhilarating. I was glad to be home.

I walked into Fit Foodies Bistro exactly at 6:00. Before I could get to the hostess stand to check in for our reservation, I saw Jai waving frantically from the bar. My cheeks burned from smiling so hard when I saw my sister. The waitress just nodded and waved me back, following close behind with menus.

"Bitch," Jai shrieked, jumping up to wrap her long, slender arms around me in a bear hug. I squeezed her back equally as hard, squealing in excited delight at seeing my sister. Bracketing both shoulders, she pushed me back, holding me at arm's length. "You done fucking disappeared on my ass!" she beamed, looking me up and down. "Bali did a body *good*, I see! You look amazing, Sis!"

"Girl, stop," I said almost bashfully. Almost... I knew she was referring to the 12 pounds I dropped in the last two months. I hadn't intentionally lost weight, but I guess when you are running behind little ones in a sweltering hot sauna known as Bali, weight loss is inevitable. I was still proud of that amazing feat though, so

I placed one hand on my hip and threw my hair over my shoulder, giving her the best Tyra Banks smize I could muster.

"I know, bitch!" I said and we both fell into a fit of laughter, hugging again. "I missed you, Jai," I continued when we finally broke our embrace.

"*Mm hmm,*" I heard behind me. I'd almost forgotten about the waitress. She politely smiled and asked, "May I show you ladies to your table?"

"Oh, girl! Yes," Jai said to the waitress while grabbing the glass of the green fruity drink she'd been sipping at the bar when I first came in. "Don't mind us. We're just catching up. I haven't seen my sister in months 'cause she's been off galivanting around the world without me," she continued while throwing an arm around my shoulder. "Lead the way, gorgeous."

She left a twenty-dollar bill on the bar before winking and blowing a kiss at the sexy, bearded bartender. I caught him blushing as he caught Jai's air kiss on that sexy-ass cheek of his.

"Alright now, Jai," I giggled. "Reagan's going to cancel the order on that next Louis, Prada, or Fendi bag I know you've been begging for if he catches you flirting like that."

"Girl, Reagan ain't gonna do shit!" she said with a giggle before innocently bringing it back to demurely clutch the literal pearls hanging around her neck. "I better calm my ass down though before he does." We both fell into a fit of laughter again. "I was just looking," she said before continuing her sashay to our table.

I grinned because I knew she would never mess up the good thing she had with her husband of 16 years. They were #relationshipgoals, and Reagan loved her dirty *stank-walk* drawers. As much as she talked shit and acted hard, she loved him, too. It always amazed me that after two whole children and several years of being married, my sister and brother-in-law could barely keep their hands off each other.

Once we settled at our table, I placed my drink order. Jai and I both studied the menu to decide what we were going to eat. It was our ritual before we both looked up at the waitress and said at the same time, "I'll have the *Kiss It.* " It was basically the only dish we ever ordered at the bistro.

All of the food there was amazing, but the decadent macaroni goodness infused with cheddar and smoked gouda topped with sundried tomatoes, gilled mushrooms, onions, and sauteed spinach was to die for. The dish was finished off with salmon, grilled to perfection, and a single prawn for garnish. We were about to be full as hell!

The waitress smiled as she looked back and forth between the two of us as if she were enjoying our reunion as much as we were. "Come here often?" she asked as she collected our menus.

"Our favorite unwind spot," Jai said as I nodded in agreement. The waitress smiled again and left to put in our orders.

Not two seconds after we were alone at the table, Jai rounded on me in her seat, resting her chin on the backs of her two manicured hands, looking at me expectantly.

"What?" I asked.

"Bitch, you know what. You come back here looking tanned, toned, and snatched. Tell me about this trip!" she said, again bugging her eyes and twisting her lips up into a pout for emphasis.

"The trip was great," I said, trying not to be weird, yet knowing she was going to see straight through my superficial answer. "Ocean breezes, beautiful weather and people. The food was pretty damn good too and dirt cheap." I couldn't stop the nostalgic smile from spreading across my face as I thought back on the beauty and peace of the island. "Oh, and before I forget," I said, turning to rummage through my tote, "I come bearing gifts."

Jai squealed in excitement at the beautiful, wooden Nefertiti earrings I had made for her in the market in Seminyak. She was equally as thrilled about the hand-woven and painted batik sarong made of raw silk. She held it up to see it better in the ambient lighting of the restaurant before crumbling it to her chest and reaching to hug me again.

She secured her gifts in her bag, then turned back to me and waved her hand under her chin in an expectant gesture. "Continue, bitch," she said eyes raised and lips pursed.

Damn. She is not going to let me off the hook.

"Ok." I rolled my eyes before continuing, "The kids were amazing, and I met some of the dopest people and made really good friends." I told her about Gro and Naija and the bond I made with them. I told her about Dominic's silly self and about Jen, Francis, and Jeff. I started telling her that my fragile ass even got on the dance floor and turned that shit out, before lowering my eyes as a thought of Kendrick crossed my mind. I quickly smiled it off and looked back up at my sister, "Mission accomplished. I took the time that I really needed to relax, relate, and release. And here I am. It was the experience of a lifetime."

"And? When you gonna tell me about the dick that has you over there holding a secret conversation with yourself."

"Girl, what?" I said, rolling my eyes as if she didn't know what she was talking about.

"Don't you 'girl what' me," she said, mocking my tone. She sat back and touched herself in the center of her chest, "I know you well, Rhi." She leaned in and whispered, "You left here looking and acting like a damn sad puppy, yet you come back here glowing and fine as fuck!" She sat back and folded her hands across her chest in checkmate fashion. "The only thing that would have a bitch losing

20 pounds and straightening her goddamned crooked-ass crown like that is some new dick you rode, conquered, and said buh-bye to."

She had my ass there.

I sat back and sighed before deciding to just tell her about him.

"Well," I said, and Jai glared at me still expectantly. "It's nothing, really. I met this guy. At first, I thought he was a douchebag, but I turned out to be wrong. He," I hesitated, trying to find the right words. "He ended up leaving abruptly and that's that." I smiled ruefully at Jai, hoping that that would satisfy her curiosity, knowing full well it wouldn't.

"So... he just bounced? Y'all at least exchanged numbers, right?" again, she looked at me expectantly.

"*Umm*. No," I said, expecting to feel a pang of sadness. But I didn't. I looked Jai right in the eye, repeating, "No. We didn't exchange numbers. I was a bit pissed at the fact that he basically ghosted me and flew back home. But, for some reason, I feel like that is how it was supposed to be."

I wasn't really thinking of the words as they flowed out of my mouth, and that—if anything—made them all the more true.

"He made me feel something I haven't felt in a long time... about myself and about romantic relationships. It didn't last, and that's fine. It was significant enough to make me realize I don't *have to* put my everything into a man to feel whole. He didn't even know it, but he helped me discover a strength within me. A beauty and ability to be myself," I paused, taking a deep breath. "And to be okay with who I am."

I looked up to see Jai's look of surprise and happiness for me.

"Ok," she nodded and began giving me a soft golf clap. "Yesss, bitch," she said and air-fived me across the table just before our food came.

We ate and continued to catch up. I was so grateful for my sister and felt lighter after telling her about Kendrick. It felt even better to know I could talk about him and our connection without feeling sad about it.

"Oh, one more thing," I said changing the subject and wriggling my eyebrows up and down excitedly. "I stopped by the office to meet with my team last week and the project is almost done."

"Damn, girl," Jai muttered between bites. "Your ass didn't waste any time getting back in the saddle."

I laughed at her comment, clasping my hands together under my chin, squeezing my shoulders up in excitement. "Stanton told me that my project was making waves in the sustainability community and there are rumors that me and my team are up for nomination for the Reuter's Annual Trailblazer Award."

"That's amazing, little sis! Now, what the fuck is that?" she said, popping the now peeled prawn into her mouth.

Chapter 33 - Kendrick

IT WAS ALMOST A full 24 hours later from the time I'd gotten the call about Ona's heart attack and my plane was touching down in Waikiki. I took an Uber straight to the hospital and the elevator straight to ICU. I was disheveled and unshaven as I barreled down the corridor to the waiting room where my baby girl waited all alone. It was moments like these that I cursed the air Jade breathed. But according to Jada, her mom had been in the wind since shortly after the last time she popped up and Ona let her stay. I nearly lost it when my little girl came barreling towards me as soon as I stepped through the door of the waiting room.

"Daddy!" she ran to me and crumpled in my arms, barely able to speak through her sobbing. "It took you so long to get here."

"I'm here now, baby," I stroked my little girl's tight coils, trying my best to comfort her.

"I was so scared, Dad," the words tumbled from her mouth. "Ona just fell, and I couldn't wake her. I didn't know what to do at first. So, I just called 911." She sobbed, placing her forehead on my arm.

The ICU nurse who led me to the waiting room was standing in the doorway and said in a soothing voice, "Your baby's a hero. Not only did she call 911 in time, she also administered CPR until the paramedics got there," she explained as I looked down in wonder at Jada.

"You did that, sweet girl?"

Jada nodded slowly, "We learned it in school. When I checked TiTi's pulse, I just started doing what we were taught."

The nurse added, "You were extremely brave and may have saved your aunt's life."

At this point the tears I'd been holding back erupted. I feebly tried wiping them away as I kissed Jada's forehead repeatedly. On the one hand, I didn't even know she knew how to do CPR and was extremely proud of her. On the other, I'd also heard the nurse say that she *may* have saved Ona's life, which spurred me to ask, "Is Ona going to be ok?"

The nurse responded, "She's not out of the woods yet. The heart attack was severe, but the emergency surgery went off without a hitch. The doctor will be able to tell you more. I'll let him know you're here." She moved back out into the hallway.

Ona was a fighter, but I still felt helpless and was scared shitless. We couldn't lose the old girl. She was my dad's oldest sister and the only family I still had remaining on the island ever since my dad died five years back. If it weren't for Ona, I don't know where Jada and I would be right now. She was the mother I never had and both a mother and grandmother to Jada.

The doctor passed by about an hour later and repeated what the nurse had already told us. The surgery went well, but Ona was still in a fight for her life. She crashed a couple of times in the three days since I'd been back and had been placed in a medically induced coma to lessen the strain on her heart.

Jada had been out of school the last three days. She was traumatized from witnessing her TiTi have a heart attack and I wanted to keep her near me. We practically stayed at the hospital, wanting to be present the moment Ona came out of the coma. Tonight, we kept to the same routine. I sat reviewing emails on my tablet, while Jada did some of the homework her teacher sent over so that she wouldn't get behind in her studies.

I heard someone enter the waiting room but didn't look up until I heard my name being called by the door, "*Ka*– Kendrick," she stammered. I looked up at the unexpected sound and almost recoiled from Jade's emaciated body as she scurried into the room.

"Jade," I gasped almost unsure it was her. Months passed since I last saw her. I knew her addiction had taken a turn for the worse, but I couldn't believe how much she had transformed. Her cheeks were hollow, and her hair looked uneven—like it had broken off on one side. I could see her flinch when she noticed me recoil. I instantly felt bad for not being able to control my shock.

Jada, who had seen her mom less than three weeks ago, also appeared to be shaken by her mother's appearance. Undaunted, Jade walked in slowly and put both hands into the pocket of her hoodie to hide the visible twitching of her hands. "Hi Jada," she said, staring with wild glassy eyes, appearing to have been up for days on end.

Jada responded with a weak wave, "Hey, Mom," moving closer to me instead of towards Jade's now outstretched hands.

Seeing that our 12-year-old daughter was frightened of her, Jade's mood shifted in an instant from an act of normalcy—as if she wasn't high as a kite on whatever her drug of choice was at the moment—to spurting venom at me in her words. "Oh... So, you're back, huh? Bet you been putting bullshit in Jada's ear that her mama ain't worth shit, again?"

"Whoa, Jade," I said, now standing to block her from Jada's view. Our baby girl was already traumatized, and I didn't need Jade showing up high with her wild accusations. From her clipped speech, sporadic movements, and this bipolar emotional swing, I surmised that she must have been fresh off of a meth binge. I'd seen her act like this before and tried to get her help. I'd be damned if she'd come up in here acting a fool, right now.

"Jada, baby, I'm going to talk to your mom outside. Stay here and wait for the doctors just in case they come in with any news about TiTi." I smiled at Jada, hoping that my voice and smile let her know that everything was okay because right now, she was shook. The smile totally left my face as I turned around and faced Jade. "You. Come. *Now.*" I stepped past her, grabbing her by the elbow to guide her out of the waiting room into the hallway. My palm easily cupped around her frail arm; I was still shocked at how thin her body was.

"Take your *gaw*-damn hands off me, Kendrick!" she yelled, trying to pull away until I yanked her right in front of me and bent to meet her eyes.

"On God, if you don't stop this foolishness in front of our daughter, I will call security and have you removed!"

She calmed after that and followed me out the door where I released her arm. "Jade, what are you doing here?" I asked as calmly as I could.

"I heard about Ona and came to get, Jada," she said, looking down at her feet in shame, not wanting to meet my eyes. "I didn't know you were back."

"Jade, I told you not to come around our daughter high."

"High?" she laughed wildly. "I didn't smoke today. I'm not high," she spat at me this time defiantly.

I was in no frame of mind to go back and forth with Jade. Again, I calmed myself as much as possible and said, "Jada is fine. I flew in three days ago as soon as I got word of Ona's heart attack. Ona is stable but they have her basically sedated to keep her stress levels low so she can recuperate faster."

It looked as if my words had satisfied Jade's need to help. She stammered, "Good. I'm glad you were here."

"Everything will be okay, but will you please go get some rest and clean up?" I implored her with my worried eyes. "Don't get me wrong... I'm glad you came, but Jada doesn't need to see you like this."

She backed away, embarrassed. She pulled on her sleeves like she was just realizing how unkept she really looked. Then, she reached a hand up and began tugging on the broken whisps of hair at the side of her head. It explained why her hair was so broken off. Apparently, whatever she was on gave her a nervous tick and she took it out on her hair when she wasn't picking at the skin around her broken, dirty nail beds.

She started walking backwards towards the elevators. Her slow movements only made her seem more suspicious; she looked like she was about to turn and run at any moment. "Jade. I'll bring her by to see you in a couple of days, okay?"

She nodded, swiping the tears that were brimming in her eyes, then she scurried down the hall.

I had to fight back nausea and my own tears. I hated to see Jade like this. And I hated the effect it had on our daughter. Jada didn't show it, but I knew it hurt her to see her mom like this. TiTi and I both tried to shield her from it, but it was an inevitable truth that Jade may be gone past the point of no return. At least she hadn't totally abandoned Jada. I felt guilty at the thought that sometimes I wished she would.

I made it back to Jada and wrapped her in my arms. We didn't talk much for the rest of the night, both of us were consumed by our own thoughts.

Rhi infiltrated mine. I felt a great sense of shame and frustration with myself. I left Bali in a hurry without enough time to leave word for her at the front desk. I only had an hour to retrieve my personal belongings from the hotel to make the last flight out for the day in order to get to Jada. And with the unfortunate series of events that transpired since my return, I was too caught up to even get in touch with Rhi.

At this point, she probably hated me all over again, rightfully so. Maybe it was better this way. A clean cut. Hell, who was I kidding. We lived on opposite ends of the country, and I was a single father of a child who she didn't even know I had. I planned on telling her about Jada, and consequently about Jade during the dinner. What woman in their right mind would want to deal with my baggage?

A couple more days went by, and Rhi was still heavily on my mind. Jada was back in school, so I was waiting alone at the hospital today. I decided to see if I could get a call through on Micah's cell phone, since the cellular service should have been restored on most of the island by now. It rang for a while. I was about to hang up when he answered.

"Yo, Kendrick," Micah's voice crackled through the line. "Good to hear from you, *brah*. We were worried. How's Ona?"

"Still a little touch and go, but Ona's a fighter," I said, not knowing if I was trying to convince him or myself.

"Amen to that, brother," I could hear relief in his voice. "And baby girl? How is she?"

"She's good, man. Went back to school today, but she was pretty shook watching her TiTi have a heart attack," I blew out a sigh. "Man, that's my baby, she shouldn't have had to see that."

"Jada's a G, man. That little *wahine* of yours is tough as nails. She's going to be fine."

"Yeah, you're right, man. She's brave as hell, too. Nurse said she may have saved Ona's life."

"Oh, yeah? See. Tough as nails," he repeated. "Jade around?"

"Nah. She popped her ass in here looking glassy-eyed the other night. Haven't seen her since," I said, now leaning against the wall, arms folded. "She's not looking too good. Back on that meth shit again."

"She didn't upset Jada, did she?" Micah asked, almost holding his breath.

"Little bit. I had to rush her out of here before she said something stupid." There was a lull in our conversation as we both processed the fact that Jade was probably gone to the drugs forever.

Stepping away from the wall, I changed the subject to work, "The project should be under wraps pretty soon, right?"

"Yep, couple more days and all of the main infrastructure will be complete. You see the cellular service is now back online?"

"Yeah. Glad I was able to get through. I need you to go over and provide Ketut with the final handoff of everything and then coordinate getting the guys and our equipment back," I stated as I ticked off my mental checklist to ensure we finalized everything.

"Too easy my man," he assured.

"*Umm*, there's one other thing," I paused.

"What's that?"

"Have you seen Rhi?" I asked nervously, clearing my throat as I waited on his response.

"Saw her a few days ago. She asked about you."

My spirits lifted at his words but were quickly doused when he added, "She left Bali, my dude."

Before I could ask him any further questions, Ona's nurse stepped into the waiting room and said, "Your aunt is awake and asking for you."

I turned back to my call and said, "Yo man, I have to go. Ona just woke up."

Chapter 34 - Rhiyan

IT HADN'T TAKEN ME long to get back into the swing of things at 3W. Two months had passed since I got back from Bali and I must admit, I missed the place and my team. Even though I stayed in contact with Stanton, Delia, and the rest of them through our weekly touchpoint calls that I refused to give up while I was away, it was good to be back in the fray.

We came a long way on the project since I'd come back on board and had been working tirelessly to wrap up construction for the grand opening of Parque Place at the Hamlet in time for the mid-November ribbon-cutting ceremony.

We pulled it off! The mayor and several well-known and local artists had come out for the grand opening weekend. Parque Place was still the talk of the town a month later. It was a big deal for the city of Atlanta. Social media content was going viral. With all the entertainment and events that went on in the city on a regular basis, the mayor and some of the very vocal pundits in the community made sure this project was well supported. The free concerts, free food, and giveaways that popped off as soon as the mayor finished her speech and cut the ribbon, drew record breaking crowds.

It was now mid-December—exactly one month after the grand opening. It was an amazing feat to pull off opening on time, but we did it. To make the accomplishment even sweeter, I had indeed been nominated for the coveted Trailblazer Award for the sustainable design of Parque Place. The property had also achieved Platinum LEED certification. And for the cherry on top, Reuters, the body nominating me for the Trailblazer Award, had chosen to host the 15th Annual Sustainability Award ceremony in the event space of the hotel in Parque Place. If I won the award, it was serendipitous that it would be presented on the very same property I was nominated for.

Just to think, less than five months ago, the project was in jeopardy of going over budget and being delayed, and I was on the verge of losing my job. Oh, how the tide had changed.

The award ceremony was tomorrow night, and we had been so busy with media engagements for Parque Place that I didn't have a chance to get a gown or shoes for the ceremony.

The name Parque Place at the Hamlet was so befitting because it truly was a mixed-use space that mimicked a small village complete with both high-end and affordable living spaces, eclectic eateries where you could grab a quick lunch or sit down for a five-star dining experience. There were fashionable boutiques that sold purses, suits, and furnishings. Anything you could buy was available here. It was only right that I shopped in one of the posh boutiques—at the place that I literally helped build—to get my ensemble for the black-tie affair.

Parque Place had something for everyone. If you weren't into shopping or eating, you could still enjoy the park which was at the center of the entire property, complete with walking and bike paths, a lake which was big enough for paddle boat rentals and a huge, man-made waterfall that was perfect for outdoor weddings or Instagram-worthy selfies.

The on-property Whole Foods, movie theater, office spaces, condos, and townhomes meant it truly was a space that you could live, play, and work in. The community gardens and makerspaces on the property rounded out the entire concept and was a major factor in my nomination for the Trailblazer Award.

My favorite part of the entire development was the skatepark. I decided to get some steps in and walk down to the vibrantly colored ramps before I got my shopping on.

As I got closer, I heard a roar of applause, *oohs* and *ahhs* coming from the direction I was heading. I walked quicker to see what was going on. There was always something exciting going down at the skatepark, which is why it was my favorite. It was a major draw for skateboarders and enthusiasts, young and old, who came from all over the city.

When I got close enough, I could see several onlookers glued to a tall, gangly girl who was on the ramps. Her curly hair billowed out of her helmet, flying behind her as she completed daring moves on the ramps. I had never skateboarded in my life, but I played Tony Hawk enough times with my nephew to know she was doing some amazing shit on that board.

At one point she paused on the ledge of the highest ramp, tipped her *Zindaya-esque* head at the onlookers with a cocky wink before leaning into the free-floating wheels at the end of her board. *Whoosh!* She was off, disappearing from my sight before emerging from the valley of the bowl to pop up and do a 360-degree spin in the air. She was so high, I could only see the wheels and the length of her board as she spun with it as a single unit against the backdrop of the sky. Her feet left the board as she landed Matrix style at the top of the ramp. The crowd went wild, and so did I!

I was so busy cheering at her performance that I didn't find it strange she was now looking at me with a big grimace on her face. Her hands grabbed at the neck of her hoody as if she was witnessing a crash. Her look of horror didn't register until she was now audibly yelling at me, "Watch out!"

And then it hit my foot and I almost tumbled forward, catching myself with one hand. I was so enthralled in her landing that I didn't pay any attention to her skateboard until it careened right into my shoe. Had she not screamed for me in warning when she did, the board would have surely broken my ankle.

The beautiful skateboarder-badass was suddenly rushing over to me, oblivious of the crowd. "I am so, so, so sorry," she yelped, helping me stand up straight.

"Oh, it's nothing!" I exclaimed to the young girl who, up-close, couldn't have been more than 13 or 14. "You were amazing out there! That was a *helluva* spin move you did!" I said enthusiastically, to assure her that I was okay more than anything.

She beamed at me with no hint of shyness at all before throwing up a hand to give me a fist bump. "I'm a badass!"

"Jada, what did I tell you about that mouth?"

The voice that chastised the young girl came from a tiny spitfire of an older woman who I hadn't noticed until now.

"Apologize *fo dah* lady," the older woman scolded the teenager, before patting my arm to also ask if I was okay. I assured her I was, then she turned back to the young girl. "You almost took her kneecaps out *wih dah* death trap you call a skateboard."

"TiTi, I already apologized," Jada whined. "She's okay! Look!" Jada rolled her eyes, sneaking me a pleading glance that made me smile.

"She apologized," I winked at Jada. "It was my fault for not watching where I was going," I said in a jovial tone. "I was telling her how amazed I was by that crazy flippity spin thing she did before you walked up." I reached out to give Jada a fist bump.

Seeing that her TiTi was satisfied with her apology, Jada wasted no time in retrieving her board. She was halfway back to the ramps as TiTi called after her, "Be careful, girl!" in an accent that sounded vaguely familiar.

"I go before she breaks a bone and I have *fo* explain *fo* her dad." She turned and began walking back after the little badass skater girl. I watched them smiling as Naija crossed my mind. The slightly older girl reminded me of her a bit. The memory made me smile as I turned to walk back towards the shops to find my dress for the ceremony.

Chapter 35 - Kendrick

"**T**HIS DRESS ITCHES ME," Jada complained.

"Stop *da* fussing and pulling before you *muss* up hair," Ona yelled back while smacking Jada's hands away from the neckline of the beautiful, silver-lined dress.

It would only take us a moment to walk over to the ballroom where the 15th Annual Sustainability Awards ceremony was getting ready to start. I tied up my polished oxfords and put on my tuxedo jacket. I was ready. The door between our adjoined rooms was ajar. As I heard Jada give Ona a fit about her dress, I knew we were going to be late.

"Ladies," I said, shaking my head as I knocked on the door jamb. "Tik-toc, we're going to be late! What are y'all doing over here?"

I walked through the room and knew they'd most likely be observing themselves in the mirror. The room looked like a tornado had blown through it—clothes across the bed, feminine appliances on the counters, Jada's skateboard and a pair of multicolored Vans on the floor, just begging for someone to make a wrong step and bust their ass. I kicked it out of the way as I made my way to the bathroom, again yelling, "Let's go!"

I stepped around the corner into the restroom opening and was winded by Jada's reflection in the mirror. Ona was standing behind her, reaching up to pull a wisp of hair that escaped the bun at the nape of Jada's neck. Jada looked down at the countertop, patiently waiting on Ona to stop fussing.

Jada was stunning. Her features mirrored her mother's before the partying, drugs, and booze, but she still had the innocence and rosy cheeks of a baby. Then I was staring into brown, golden flecked eyes that matched mine in the mirror. She caught my unguarded look of a father realizing for the first time that his baby was growing into a beautiful young lady right before his eyes.

True to form, she licked out her tongue, turning the sentimental moment into pure comedy with her quick wit, "I know you're not about to cry, Dad!" she burst out laughing, and I smiled.

Not letting her get away with mocking my proud Dad moment, I responded, "Nah, little lady. I just know that this may be the only time I'll get to see you in a dress. Better yet, smell you smelling like a girl," I fanned my nose for emphasis.

"*Ooh*, funny," she said, giving me a silly face and goofy laugh before breaking free of Ona's grip and sweeping past me to put on the ballerina flats that matched her dress to perfection. I was going to have to fight like hell to keep her riding skateboards and wearing Chucks and hoodies for as long as I could. *Get the shotgun ready.*

"TiTi, you did good getting this tom-boy beat into shape," I said, hugging my auntie. I side stepped the mess in Jada's room and held out an elbow to each of my dates for the night, and we walked out the door. "Let's go get this dog and pony show over."

We were now seated in the opulent auditorium at one of the many tables in a sea of white linen tops and patrons dressed to the nines in tuxes and evening gowns. I scanned the room taking in the full elegance of it all. This was a huge event for the construction, engineering, architectural and other adjacent industries to be recognized not only for the size, scale, and creativity of the work we did, but specifically for how we did the amazing work while trying to be responsible corporations as well. Kekoa Industries won the coveted Trailblazer Award a few years back, so it was pretty awesome to be nominated again in a different category.

Ona's cackling laugh at something she and Jada had obviously been chatting about broke in my reverie. "You need *fo* scan *da* room *fo* find Cinderella in this bougie-ass ballroom," she chuckled at the narrowing of my eyes when I caught on to what she was saying. "Jada and me ran into pretty little *wahine* down *da* skatepark while you were out galivanting *da* city yesterday."

"First of all, I wasn't galivanting... I was working. Second, who were you bothering at the skatepark?" I stared back at her, giving the same sassiness back to her, mimicking the bugged eyes she was giving me and trying not to laugh at the fake clutching of her pearls as she acted wounded.

"Me? I *no boddah* no one..." she smiled like she was hiding a secret. "Your *keiki* just almost took the kneecaps out from under *da* most beautiful, tall, woman. Nevermind, she isn't your type anyway."

"What do you mean not my type?"

"Yeah, Dad, she might be too much for you to handle," Jada chimed in, giving her TiTi a high-five across the table. "You know you *like 'em* a little less refined."

"What?" I said caught off guard by my little girl telling me about the type of woman I liked. She giggled before saying, "I've seen those half-wits you try to sneak out before the sun comes up, I may be thirtee-"

"In two days!" I cut her off.

"Not the point," she continued. "I ain't slow."

I was a bit crest-fallen and felt like I'd been caught in the act. She saw the look on my face and quickly followed up with, "*Aww*, I'm sorry, Dad. It's cool. I know you're not getting back with Jade... But you need to find somebody. TiTi and I are sick of you working all the time and being grumpy. You need to get you some boot-"

"Hey!" I cut her off, silently thanking God for the distraction the waiter brought when he asked if he could take our drink orders.

I turned back to the stage as the award show fully kicked off and the first sets of nominees were being announced.

After about 40 minutes of being regaled with stories about the latest tech innovations and backstories about social, economic, and environmentally responsible corporations, the time of the evening had come for one of the biggest awards, the Trailblazer Award.

The announcer went through a touching story about a company from right here in Atlanta, GA, laying out the amazing developmental effort that they planned and orchestrated with many civic and municipal organizations to create a space that embodied southern culture intertwined with arts, economy, and sweeping green spaces—an intersection of business, shopping, relaxing, and good food—in one sustainable center that would cater to every appetite and desire of the citizens of Atlanta and the world. The announcer praised the work in such a way that everyone was on the edge of their seat waiting to hear the winner.

"And the winner of the 15th Annual Trailblazer Award goes to a leader in sustainable design, architecture and the developer of the very hotel and event space we all sit in right now," he paused dramatically. "Rhiyan Carson of Wiley, Whitman and White!"

Wait. Did he just say... It felt as if the air had been sucked from the room when I saw her stand up in what seemed like slow motion. Her ascension up the stairs in the beautiful black satin dress that grazed the curves etched into my memory felt like a dream. She began to give her acceptance speech as I sat there in dazed silence, missing the standing ovation that she received.

"Hey, look TiTi, that's her!" Jada said, totally fan-girling and clapping excitedly in her seat along with everyone else in the room. I thought of her non-stop since the day I'd left Bali over two months ago. I even tried to find her on social media, but there was no trace of her. Then Jada's words hit me.

"Wait, how do you know her?"

Jada and TiTi both turned to me and said, "That's her, the lady from the skatepark."

I was floored. My eyes and thoughts were back on Rhi. We'd never gotten to talk about what she did for a living. I knew she lived in Atlanta, but that was about the extent of it. She was finishing up her acceptance speech, about to leave the stage when it hit me. *Go to her.*

She raised the award triumphantly before elegantly walking backstage. I knew that this may be my only chance to ever talk to her again. "I'll be right back," I said, standing abruptly and making my way out the door to the elevator that would take me to the mezzanine, where I knew all award recipients would go for post-victory pictures.

I made it off the elevator in time to see her posing for the first picture. She'd been joined by another young lady that shared a striking resemblance. Different skin tones but matching eyes.

The photo shoot was concluded, and she prepared to walk away with her companion. Her back was to me as I walked up behind her, silently begging the lady that shared her eyes to not say anything.

"You clean up pretty well, Rhi," I whispered as close to her ear as I could. Her back stiffened and I braced for a slap—a move I would willingly take if it meant I got to feel her touch again. It didn't come and she didn't turn around.

I couldn't see her face. Whatever the expression, it alerted the other woman that something was wrong. Rhi continued to stand with her back to me, but the other lady, she went into straight up protection mode.

"Who the fuck are you?" she asked, pulling Rhi away as she stepped between us. She handed her clutch to the man who was also standing there who I noticed for the first time. He stood there with more surprise on his face than I had on mine as the woman prepared to square off with me. All the while, Rhi stood there still as a frigid pole—in total shock.

Had it not been for the man, who was obviously with the wild-eyed lady and Rhi placing a calming hand on the small of her back and grabbing the elbow of the arm that was about to swing, I might have been sporting a black eye tomorrow.

At this point Rhi's eyes were locked on mine, but her face was passive. "Kendrick."

The twin looked back and forth between Rhi and me. "Kendrick?" She kept looking back and forth. "The *fuck-boy* from Bali, Kendrick?"

Rhi's perfectly arched eyes raised high, and her head nodded almost imperceptibly in my direction as if to say, 'Yeah.'

I deserved that.

"Rhi, *umm*," I paused, words failing me. I started again, but this time directing my attention to the two onlookers. I reached out my hand to the feisty one first and said, "I'm Kendrick. Kendrick Kekoa. Rhi and I met in Bali."

The woman didn't take my hand; she let it dangle there between us as she grilled me menacingly. The guy shook it instead, quelling some of the awkwardness.

"Reagan, man. Reagan Philmore… and this is my wife, Jai'Elle," he looked down at her. Her narrowed eyes never left mine. He gently placed his hands on his wife's shoulders and squeezed them to ease some of the tension. It appeared to be working as she slowly rolled her eyes away from mine and up into her husband's. He said directly to her in a hushed tone, "Looks like they have some catching up to do. Let's give these two some space."

Acquiescing to her husband's urging, the still hostile woman moved to the side, but not before saying, "Sis, we'll be right over here if you need us." She gave me a final sneer before reluctantly allowing her husband to steer her away. *Damn, I thought Rhi was feisty, but she has nothing on Sis.*

When we were alone, I chanced catching Rhi's eyes and reached for her hand. She quickly pulled it away when she hissed, "Don't fucking touch me, Kendrick."

"I'm sorry," I said, never taking my eyes off her face.

"Yeah," she said and for the first time, looked into my eyes, "I know." Her anger was palpable. "I shed tears… opened up to you about my divorce. I trusted you with my emotions, and you couldn't even say goodbye."

Her eyes looked blank, but I saw her fight the urge to cry; her cool resolve stiffened her spine, and she didn't let a single tear drop. I rubbed a hand across my face to calm my own nerves and settled on the only thing I knew to do in this moment and repeated, "I am so sorry, Rhi. Please allow me to explain."

"Explain?" she said incredulously. "Now you want to explain?" she threw up her hands in exasperation and walked over to the balcony to look down into the lobby. Her hands gripped the railing, tendons bulging in her knuckled grip. I still affected her.

I walked up behind her, not so close that we were touching, but enough to invade her personal space.

"I tried to call you, but you had already checked out."

"Really? I didn't check out until three days after our last night together. Try again," she huffed.

"I know. Rhi, there is so much I need to tell you, and the original plan was to let you know at dinner." She moved away from me. I followed, adamant to clear my conscience. "I have a daughter."

"Surprise!" she hissed sarcastically. "That much I already know. Unfortunately, I found out that small detail from your dear friend, Micah."

"Something happened and I had to rush home."

"That's it," she said, hands now on her hips. "Something happened... and... you couldn't come tell me?" she questioned in absolute disbelief.

"There wasn't any time," I said, speaking faster as she began to walk away. "Look, I had to leave my daughter with my aunt. Ona had a heart attack, and my daughter was there when it happened. She's only 12, Rhi. There was no time!" I implored her to hear me. "I only had an hour to make it to the hotel, grab my things, and get to the airport. I dropped everything! I'm sorry... but that included you. Before I knew it, the days flew by. Baby, I swear I called... but you had left Bali."

I'd been fighting back my own tears when the gravity of it all hit me again as I tried to explain the circumstances to Rhi.

"I didn't want to leave you, baby," I said, allowing the words to sit between us. "I had no choice."

She didn't say anything, just took a few steps closer, placing her palm on my cheek. Her eyes had softened a bit.

"I thought you just left. I had no idea about your daughter until Micah told me. He didn't share any of this, just that you left, and I didn't question it. Why didn't he tell me?" she said, tears now brimming in her eyes. "And a daughter. You have a daughter. Why didn't *you* tell me that?"

"It's what I planned to share with you at dinner," I said apologetically.

The tears were now slowly streaming down her face. "The dinner never came." She closed her eyes tightly, head succumbing to the force of gravity with the realization that I hadn't intentionally hurt her.

I closed the gap between us and pulled her into my chest. I whispered, "I love you, Rhiyan Carson," then crushed her lips with mine. We stayed there in that embrace. Time seemed to stop until I heard Jada's voice from the direction of the elevators.

"Daddy! There he is, TiTi." Rhi tried to step back, a questioning look on her face, but I pulled her closer.

When TiTi and Jada got closer and realized the scene of me holding a woman under my arm, they both froze.

Rhi broke the silence first, looking between Jada and me then to TiTi, "You're the badass skater from the park yesterday."

"And you *da* beautiful *wahine* that we told Kendrick about," Ona smiled slightly, then winked at Jada. "Maybe she not out his league after all."

"Wait. *This* is your daughter?" Rhi asked looking back and forth between Jada and me.

"Yes, this is my little tom-boy. Jada, I'd like you to meet Rhi."

Jada smiled impishly, "Dad, you're late, we met yesterday. This is the lady from the skate park that we told you about."

Titi Ona questioned, "Hold up. How *you two* know each *uddah*?"

"We met in Bali," Rhi and I said in unison giving each other a quick look.

"Well, well, well!" Ona clapped both hands to her face, "You must done more than met in Bali," she grinned. "You got my nephew's nose so wide open; he chase *af* you and missed his whole *'ward* presentation!" She held out the small golden trophy to Kendrick, tsking. "This *heathun* actually won and wasn't there *fo* do his own acceptance speech... Well, TiTi Ona had you covered *kane*!" Ona said as Jada scowled in embarrassment.

"Dad, she went on stage and accepted the award for you... even told them about how she used to whip your butt when you were a little boy. So embarrassing!" Jada fumed while everyone around her, including Rhi's sister, burst out laughing.

Ona then turned to Rhi, her smile lines creasing her eyes and mouth, and said, "Ha, you *da* one he pine over for *da* last couple of months." She reached up and touched Rhi's cheek, "I can see *why*."

Rhi looked up into my eyes, then back at Ona and Jada, "Would you two do me the honor of joining me for a celebration dinner?" She paused to look at me, "Oh, and your dad, too."

Epilogue – Rhiyan

T HE BALMY, YET WARM night breezes brushed my naked skin as I stood in the opening of the French doors leading to the balcony outside Kendrick's bedroom. He looked like a bronzed god in the shadowy glow of oil lamps that resembled tiki torches on the deck. Without turning around, he growled in a low voice over the slow 90's R&B that was playing on the surround sound, "Bring your sexy ass here, Rhi."

I wasted no time, making my way to him. I slipped my arms around his waist to press my body against the length of his back, gasping when my hand grazed the hardness of his dick.

"Baby, really?" I giggled, "We just finished... and you're ready again?"

"I'm always ready for your sweet, wet, pussy," he said, turning around slowly and punctuating each word with a kiss to my lips.

"I love it here," I said, giggling as his lips tickled the sensitive area just above my collarbone. I reached to pull his lips to mine for another kiss.

"And I love you, Mrs. Kekoa" Kendrick responded.

This time, I was ready for him and wrapped my legs around his waist when he scooped me into his arms and carried me to the bed. "I love you more, Mr. Kekoa," I whispered in a moan as he sank into my slick wetness before my back even hit the pillowtop.

It had been a full year since the award ceremony, and my now husband and I were reunited. We had just gotten back from our honeymoon a week ago. Jada spent the weekend with Ona, giving us a few more days to explore our new life as husband and wife before school started back after the Christmas break.

We decided that our primary home would be in Hawaii so as Jada's routine would not be disrupted, but we also maintained my condo in Atlanta because we both had to travel there often for work. It turned out that Kekoa Industries was selected as the lead civil and structural engineering firm to do a full assessment of all major bridges and interchanges in the city after the I-85 debacle.

The transition was easy for me as well because I could work remotely at 3W, only needing to fly in for important events.

We tried dating long distance but realized we couldn't handle the distance apart six months in. It was easy enough getting to each other because flights flew between Atlanta and Hawaii all the time. The problem was that neither of us ever wanted to leave to go home. Kendrick actually popped the question right before rushing through security to make his flight.

I had gotten to know Jada and Ona very well. I even met Jade a few times and fell in love with all of them, even her. She still had her demons, but I could see glimpses of a beautiful woman with a beautiful spirit beneath her hardened exterior. Our relationship was naturally rocky at first. I was the new woman. What ex-partner wouldn't have a problem with that? But it didn't take long for me to see that she was only worried about Jada and wanted the best for her. I think her worries subsided when she believed I would grow to love her daughter unconditionally.

And Jada. Well, let's just say, I never met a more friendly, sweet girl in my life. I was happy to have the privilege of being her bonus mom. She and Ona kept me in stitches.

Jai'Elle eventually fell in love with her new brother-in-law and actually planned our entire wedding in Atlanta; she even had a spread about us in one of the magazines she represented.

We were a blended family. I picked up a bonus mom too, in Ona, and Kendrick a bonus dad, sister, brother-in-law, niece, nephew, and a host of aunts, uncles and cousins in my extended family. Life wasn't perfect, but it was ours, and we made the best out of it together.

The End

Thanks for reading Bali Blue. Will you please leave a review on Amazon at the link below.

Leave a Review: amzn.to/4dE4Bl4

Excerpt from Mess on the Mara

Prologue — Andra

"**A**NDRA!" MY MOM YELLED from the bottom of the staircase. "Bring your ass lil' girl, you can't miss the bus today. I have to go to the studio and can't be late! Got a new artist to meet with!"

My momma yelling was nothing new. Her normal morning voice was a shout and typically stayed in a shout until either I did what she was prompting me to do or if the phone rang and she had to turn on her work voice. Then of course she usually stayed in soft spoken, calm collected art curator voice until the next morning and the yelling started all over again.

"I'm coming, "I yelled back as I swiped on the bubble gum pink lip gloss and took a final look at my baggy jeans, mock crop top and matching pink and white Retro 1s but it was the sound of the school bus coming over the hill that lit the fire under my butt to get downstairs and out the door. Grabbing my book bag, I bounded down the steps two at a time, planting a kiss on my mom's cheek making sure to miss her signature bright red lipstick as I passed her on the way out the door. I ran down the block to the corner to catch the school bus. On the way, noticing the big U-Haul truck that was pulled up on the curb blocking half the sidewalk, making me have to step off the curb to go around it, almost getting my shoes dirty! I had Mr. Washington's class during first block this morning and the folks moving into the big empty house at the corner of Wadley and Tiger Flowers Drive were about to make me mess up my fresh!

Per usual, I walked into my Wednesday 7th grade pre-algebra class, perfectly timed to make a grand entrance just before the late bell, making sure to bend over and dust off the imaginary dirt on my Jays. Drawing the exact attention I was looking for from the fellow sneaker heads in my class and just before Mr. Washington closed the door signaling to anyone who was late to keep right on past to the office to get a tardy slip.

I took my seat right in front of Mr. Wash's desk ready to discuss last night's homework assignment. It was a little hard, so I'm sure I was the only one in class who completed it and correctly. I pulled out my work and was geeked in anticipation of my favorite teacher's attention.

He was so cool and actually talked to us instead of down to his students. He got us. He got me. He made math so fun! So, I took extra care with my homework because of that... Well and because I loved being the teacher's pet and the recipient of most of his attention during class. When he said stuff like, "If you had paid attention yesterday during my lesson like Andra, you would have gotten a higher score on that quiz," it made me smile and I usually sat up straighter. Or when he'd say, "Andra, go ahead and take a nap, while everyone else takes these notes, because you got it the first time around," I'd put my head down but mainly to daydream about him. Everyone else in the class would be so jealous and I ate it up.

Even though I was his clear favorite, everyone loved Mr. Wash. Unlike most teachers, Mr. Washington took a hands-on approach to teaching. He often related our math lessons to things us 7th graders cared about. For instance, how the gamers in the class could increase the amount of time they can play video games in a day if they understand how to control the variables such as sleep, chores, homework, and school that may eat up their time. For me, he related fractions and variables to my passion for food and cooking and how the math concepts could be used for scaling recipes. He was the first teacher who took an interest in me so I was even more stoked to share how the homework helped me tweak the recipe for the batch of chocolate chip cookies that I planned to make tonight and share with the class tomorrow.

But Mr. Washington wasn't standing at the board. Nor did he make the announcement that typically came for everyone to take out their homework. Instead, he sat at his desk with a sad look on his face. I wanted to blurt out, "Mr. Wash, what's wrong," but I didn't. Just sat there looking confused like everyone else in the class.

When he finally stood, edging around to sit at the corner of his desk facing us, he clasped his hands in front of him and took a deep sigh, before giving us the most pitiful smile I'd ever seen. "Class," he said pausing as if contemplating his next words, and then the most awful thing fell out of his mouth. "Today is my last day teaching at McCullom Charter School."

What? Surely, I must have heard him wrong... I totally blacked out for a second trying to figure out how I had misunderstood what Mr. Washington said. I was so busy trying to recreate his sentence that he was way down the line of what he was trying to get across by the time I tuned back into his words – "I am getting married," he smiled ruefully like a little boy, "and will be moving to Seattle, Washington to be with my fiancée who is there finishing up law school."

This time, I audibly gasped. I hadn't misheard him. He was leaving. And before I could stop them, big boulder sized tears threatened to spring from my eyes as a knot grew, constricting my throat. I'm not sure how long I sat there tuned all the way out of what Mr. Washington was saying. Who was going to give me new ways to split up my recipes. What other teacher could possibly make me feel seen like Mr. Wash did. No one. I wanted to scream shut up at him. Tell him to go on and leave, we didn't care. I didn't care. I was pissed. Felt like my heart was pounding in my chest, threatening to rip right through it. Why was my heart hurting so bad... As soon as the bell rang, I sprang to my feet, grabbing my book bag but not caring that I left that stupid homework assignment fluttering to the floor as I made a mad dash out of his class.

At this point I could hardly see past the tears that were streaming down my face now. I inwardly groaned as I tried to rush past the throng of students that were quickly filling up the hallway to get to their next class. I ran blindly to the bathroom not looking up until I run into a wall of students blocking the door to the bathroom. It was a circle of them. Some laughing. Others shaking their head and pointing. There were a lot of ooohs and chants to stop, while others were like, who is that ugly boy, pointing at the new kid.

My anger was already at its peak because I couldn't get into the bathroom to check the tears that were now streaming down my face, but it hit white hot when I pushed through the crowd, to see Charles Ansley lunge at the skinniest boy I'd ever seen before pushing him hard making him and his book bag hit the floor and slide to the far side of the crowd that had formed.

When Charles yelled, "Get up you black African booty scratcher," I saw red. I ran at him so fast knocking that coward off his feet. I then blacked out and started wailing on him; kicking and screaming, "Call him that again! I bet you won't you bug ugly bully!" I kept swinging until I felt someone big and strong yank me off him by my book bag. Even while up in the air, I was still kicking and screaming and trying to rip that mean look off Charles Ansley's face. I locked eyes with the little skinny, dark-skinned boy, who gave me a nod of thanks. I gave him a quick grin before being drug down the hall to the principal's office by the nape of my neck.

The only reason that I didn't get suspended for fighting was because Mr. Washington told the principal that I was defending the new kid, Kobena or something like that was his name. Thank God it was Mr. Washington who broke up the fight. Because my mom was going to kill me if I had gotten suspended. What I didn't know was Mr. Washington had also explained to the principal that he'd told his class today was his last day and I didn't take it too well. Another reason why I shouldn't be suspended. The principal, however, did tell me this and explained how hard it could be to lose a great teacher and mentor such as Mr. Washington and she understood how sad and scary that could be. When I started crying again, she actually hugged me, shushing me calmly while promising it was going to be okay and that Mr. Wash would come back to visit when he could. She let me stay in her office the rest of the school day until it was time to get back on the bus to go home.

On the bus, I sat there staring out the window. The tears had long since dried but still felt some kind of way about losing my favorite teacher who I'd had a secret crush on the whole school year. I was so deep in my thoughts that I didn't notice the new boy trying to get my attention to ask if he could sit by me. I snapped back to present and stammered, "Yeah. You cool."

He took his seat then said, "I'm Kobena. Everyone calls me Kobe though," in the thickest but most interesting accent I'd ever heard. Turned out, Kobe, his bother Kenji who was already in high school and their mom and dad were the new family that moved in on my street! When we got to our block, Kobe invited me in to meet his mother and I was too excited to do so, especially when I smelled the wonderfully weird aroma of something cooking and coming from their house as soon as we got off the bus!

Mrs. Abara welcomed me into their massive home and made me and Kobe take a seat at the island in their kitchen then proceeded to fix us both the biggest and best bowls of oxtail stew over rice and beans I'd ever tasted. Years would go by with me and my best friend Kobe eating, cooking and telling jokes with his family around this island. Turned out Kobe and his family were from Accra, Ghana and when I told them that my father was Kenyan, they welcomed me in like family. Me and Kobe became the best friends ever, bonded over culture and food!

Chapter 1 – Andra

"**K**OBE!" I SQUEALED WITH pure joy. "You see this shit?" I yelled into my phone as I watched him on the shared screen of the IG live. As we sat waiting for our impromptu session to get started, the number of viewers steadily went up!

"Yeah, Boi," he said, white toothed smile beaming, slow strong claps belying his controlled excitement. "This is wild. Thirty-two thousand viewers already in the room...?" he said more as a disbelieving question rather than a statement even though we both were watching the numbers go up. "And we still have three minutes before go time!"

Our IG lives were always lit, but the fact that it was looking like a D-Nice jam session during the pandemic was surreal as fuck.

"Yoooooo! Keep on coming in the room," I said, hyping up the newcomers. Apparently, it worked because the chat was on fire, too. The energy in the room was contagious. "I know it was last minute but y'all showing the fuck out! We are so excited for y'all to join us today!" I genuinely was in awe at how many of our followers came through as heart emojis flew across the screen.

"You reading these comments, Andra_B?" Kobe asked, speaking directly to me over the video feed, "We got some of our A1's online with us today!"

"PERIOD!" I made sure my response popped swag and dripped flavor for entertainment of our followers. "You know we got some ride or dies at Gastrafrique!" I squinted at my small screen, moving in closer to shout out some folks and read a few comments from the chat out loud. "Thank you, Daddy_B_Right!" I smiled coyly, replacing the "D" sound in his name to seductively call him Zaddy.

@Daddy_B_Right: Can't wait to see what the dynamic duo has to share with us tonight

@69Flavors_CreamPie: @Chef_Ko_Bae I hope whatever y'all sharing t'night includes you taking that damn shirt off!!!

@MzLeisha_Q: I 2nd that emotion

@Afrobeats_Live123: Nah we trying to get @Andra_B to show off them #goodknees again in like she did outside @theselectatl in that sexy as LBD last weekend

@ food_porn_minaj : Yess... that food had her ass all the way turnt. GOING FOR SUNDAY BRUNCH with my girls!

"Oooh, Kobe! They lit-lit" I said staring dead into his eyes, wicked gleam in mine before gently egging him. "You taking your shirt off for the 'gram tonight, my boi?" I giggled when he shrugged his lips at me, giving dead pan face. That and it would be mighty hard for him to pull that tight ass, black turtleneck over his perfectly chiseled chest and arms on camera.

"You know… I just might take this muhfuckah off," he said, turning the dead pan for me off, turning on pure dark-chocolate charisma for our viewers continuing, "If they keep this good energy going." The chat once again exploding heart, eggplant and fire emojis.

"Alright, alright! It's 7 p.m.," I said with a bit more composure into the camera. Definitely not hating, but it was time to announce our good news and break up some of the parties happening in our females' and probably a few men's panties. "I'm sure all these good working folks are ready to hear why we wanted them on this last minute live. You ready to get this thang started Kobe?"

"Yep, yep. Let's do this shit," he said sitting back in his seat, relaxed posture, fingers steepled and looking like sex personified. I watched him talk to the audience in amazement. I knew my bestie like the back of my hand though and knew he was almost bursting at the seams with excitement because his west African accent, most times barely noticeable, was on full showcase tonight.

"First," he continued, "Shout out to the big homie @Daddy_B_Right in the comments. My G, you've been one of our biggest supporters since the beginning of Gastrafrique! It's because of dedicated followers like you sharing your heritage with us, that inspires us to share our fusion blend of African American... I mean true African American, me from Ghana and Andra with her ties to East Africa, we get to share our blended heritage and love of Afro-fusion cuisine with you..." Kobe's words trailed as he looked proudly over at me.

I picked up where he left off.

"Without further ado, we are so very proud to announce Gastrafrique has grown to five million followers on IG, surpassing the number of followers not just for BIPOC founded food blogs, but of all food blogs in every genre in the United States. Cheers to all of us African-Food Freaks!"

I paused for effect, as Kobe fist pumped causing another flurry of emojis.

"We out here competing with the likes of Gordon Ramsey and shit!" he said, "And you guys know that with that kind of fanfare, and we wouldn't have been able to do it without all y'all, we are celebrating the multitude of sponsorship offers now coming in to sponsor @Gastrafrique." Again, he paused and looked over at me to continue.

"We are now," my hands bull horning my words before throwing my arms up in field goal position, "Brand ambassadors for Condenaste! Link in bio BITCHES!"

"Yep. You heard right. Click the link in our bio for a special discount code for 25% off every luxury restaurant brand in the Condenaste network courtesy of Gastrafrique"

"And that's not all!" I yelled glad for the 360-degree swiveling auto tripod for my phone that tracked my movements as I jumped to my feet for the next part of our announcement. My drip had to be on full display for this and I did a full spin for the camera, struck a pose, and continued. "We are also now brand ambassadors for Ivy Paaaaarrrrrrrkkk," I screamed and the chat went literally apeshit!

Who would have known Gastrafrique, a little old Instagram page imagineered by me and my best friend Kobe over 10 years ago in his mom's kitchen after she'd taught us how to make fufu would be this big today? This was back when you could only post pictures on Instagram and Baby, pictures we took. Our very first post was of that fufu, along with the full recipe in the comments. That post alone got five hundred likes. Definitely not viral, but impressive enough to light a spark.

We sat down on his mom's couch for hours and racking our brains over what to call our page. All we cared about back then was capturing a good vibe and our love of all things African cuisine. And Instagram is where we chose to display it. Apparently, our followers felt the vision.

Our next three posts were from the same night. One was a picture of me in a velour Baby Phat sweatsuit pounding yam into a big wooden bowl. The next was of Mrs. Abara in an Ankara print headwrap giving me culinary direction. The last was of Kobe in a yellow Viktor Ikpeba soccer jersey, face rankled in pure bliss as he taste-tested the fufu he'd used to finger the delicious collard greens Kobe's mom made for dinner. Ten years and five million followers later, Gastrafrique was just getting started.

Today, our friendship was as tight as ever. We'd virtually grown up together on social media. Me, as Andra_B, socialite and food blogger extraordinaire. Kobe, 'aka' Chef_Ko_Bae, 'aka' Chef Kobe Abara, known internationally by his contemporaries as head Chef of one of Atlanta's only two Michelin Star restaurants, Jah.

Somewhere along our journey, we began making money from various sponsorships. No longer using our own money to eat at and critique four and five start restaurants and other hotspots around town. Now these establishments were paying us for simply trying their food and talking about it on our lit IG lives. Tonight, we'd moved into the big leagues and our followers were celebrating right along with us.

My phone rang, pulling me out of the trip down memory lane as I put the finishing touches on my makeup. I wasn't surprised to see Kobe's face lighting up the screen.

"What's good, Bestie!" I answered on the first ring, "That shit was crazy right?"

"Hell yeah! I wasn't surprised though. Free swag from Ivy Park... man sheesh... them followers came the fuck up!"

"Right," I said nodding my head in agreement and still beaming with pride for what we'd accomplished, "Daddy_B_Right was the first to join as usual. Glad we were able to shout him out."

"For sho'. I recognized several of our regular followers front and center tonight," Kobe stated as I swapped my everyday gold hoop earrings for diamond pendants to accentuate my exposed neck and draw attention to the tattoo of Africa behind my right earlobe not realizing Kobe had disconnected the call until I received an incoming video alert from the Google Meets app. A common occurrence between us because I had an Android... Not compatible with FaceTime. The video came on just as I was putting the finishing touches on the high-bun of golden brown, ass-length braids I'd somehow wrestled on top of my head.

"Damn girl, you done switched up your do that quick? Cool, I was thinking we could go over to Mom's house and keep the celebration going -" He stopped mid-sentence as I pursed my lips to apply Ruby Wu lipstick. "Never mind, I see you putting on your 'fuck-girl' lips. Who's the mark tonight?"

"Um, first off watch ya' mouth," I said. One perfectly bejeweled fingernail raised to cut him off. "Second, same dude that took me to The Select for dinner under the most Instagram-able indoor garden bar last weekend. This time, I paused long enough to stand to tug the legs of the impossibly short black leather shorts down to a respectable level, knowing full well that as soon as I started walking my thick thighs would send them back into the crevices of my ass cheeks. I turned back to finish addressing Kobe. "Dinner with that mark and the subsequent review of that bar is what got us to five million followers."

"Ahhh, Andra I'm about a-thousand-percent sure it was that lil' ass dress you were twerking in at said bar that got us over that milestone."

"Well, these red lips... these black leather shorts," I said while propping my phone up so he could see just how scandalous they were, "And these 4-inch red bottoms is about to get us at least a million more when I post this review of Prime Steakhouse tomorrow night!"

Kobe long sucked his teeth at that.

"You know we got endorsement deals now, baby girl. You don't need to be out here scamming nigga's no more."

"Welp," I giggled at his light-hearted jab, "A girl can never forget where she comes from... And guess what?"

"What Andra?" he asked, a deep V forming between his raised brows.

"You never know, this one might be a keeper. Second date and all..."

At that, his face relaxed and he folded over, laughing.

"Yeah right, this nigga bout to get took for a $600 dollar meal and stuck with blue balls..."

"And on that note, Bestie, I'm about to be late. Let's set up a real celebration at your Mom's Saturday night. You know she is just as much the reason for our success as we are! Love you boy. Gotta go!" I blew a kiss and hung up.

On my way to the restaurant, I thought back on what Kobe had said. Of course, I knew I didn't need anybody to fund my restaurant ventures anymore. Hell, most of our meals were comped by the establishments in advance because they knew great service and great food would get them a great review on Gastrafrique! But I really didn't give a fuck about these no-good ass niggas. Half of them was playing musical pussy all up and down I-75, while the other half were out here with secret families at home. The worst were the ones out here flexing on their coins, screaming for a girl like me to come pocket check'em. Damn if I wasn't going to help run it up and let them pay the tab. More accurately, pay me. Hince Kobe's reference to me scamming niggas. Not the case at all. I was great company. The spots I chose were always a top-notch experience. I always made sure to book at every restaurant and always pre-arranged that whatever he paid would be refunded back to me by the restaurant at the pre-determined compensation rate.

Seduce and mutherfuckin' scheme these niggas was more like it! I laugh at the Rap Shit reference.

Keland, my date and rookie running back just signed to the Falcons, would get treated no different. Well, maybe a little different. We'd been getting to know each other for about three weeks now, longer than most have lasted. We were going on our second official date. A girl had needs. He was six feet of big, solid copper deliciousness. He act right, I just might give him the draws for celebration's sake. I weighed the idea of having this man blow my back out against dealing with a grown ass baby pouting in the a.m. when I inevitably sent him on his way... Back shots was winning. A bullshit story about 'it's me, not you...' or 'sorry but I'm just not ready for more' would have to do the trick to get rid of him before morning. I was pulling up to valet by the time I'd made the internal decision to invite him up for drinks after dinner.

The shrill ringing of my phone was threatening to pierce my eardrum. I didn't want to risk pulling the cover from over my head, for fear that daylight would pierce my eyeballs. My right arm felt like led as I reached blindly towards the nightstand to pull the offensive piece of steel and glass under the cover to peak at the screen. As I was reaching, a broad arm reached around my waste and pulled me firmly towards the warmth of his body at the center of the bed.

"Whoa," I grunted, brain fully on alert now as the too much Ace of Spades and Coke induced cloud began to evaporate. Placing a firm hand on Keland's chest, I halted his attempt at a good morning kiss, opting to roll to the edge of the bed to answer my phone. "I have to take this," I whispered over my shoulder hoping he'd get the point. He didn't.

"Hello," I said in a hushed voice. It was Kobe.

Sounding like he'd been up for hours, Kobe greeted me in his usual boisterous baritone, tinged with Ghanaian slang, "Andra B, wake ya' ahsss' up gul! We gots more celebrat'un to do!"

Before I could pull the phone away from my ear away from Kobe's too loud voice, I had to quickly tuck it under my arm so he wouldn't hear Keland's loud ass whine, trying to sweet talk me back under the covers. Hell no! This nigga was definitely going to have to go with this shit. He did not have main nigga privileges to let his presence be known. For all he knew, my main nigga could have been on the other line. He was definitely about to get the talk and booted up out of here.

I placed the phone back to my ear in time to hear Kobe, whisper yelling, "Andra... I know damn well you did not let that lame nigga stay the night."

I hesitated before responding, looking over my shoulder at my bed mate. Stalling.

"That's none of your business. What's up and why are you calling me so damn early in the morning?" I hissed, eyes squeezing shut to stave off the impending headache.

"Morning? Andra, its noon." Shit. Noon? Definitely too much Ace of Spades last night. And why did he have to yell.

Kobe continued, "I just got an interesting call and I think you need to come to the crib ASAP!"

"Just tell me –"

"Get rid of the cornball and bring ya' ahss, Andra!"

CLICK. He hung up before I could make further argument. *Rude!* On second thought, he'd just given me the best excuse to get rid of ol' boy.

"Hey... I'm so sorry," I put on my best soft girl seasoned voice, training my features to wide-eyed apology mode before turning to face Keland on the bed, "But I have an emergency work situation with my partner that I need to go take care of." Oscar worthy performance if I did say so myself.

About the Author

CHER TERAIS IS THE ultimate Renaissance woman! With a passion for travel and an eye for gorgeous interior design and architecture, she's crafted beautiful stories centered around black love and its complexities.

Take a journey with her from busy street markets to distant escapes in her books that will take you around the world.

Originally from Warner Robins, Georgia, Cher spent time in the Army before moving to the Middle East as a Program Manager. Her travels allowed her to dive into diverse cultures as well as serve as a springboard for more trips around Asia, the Caribbean and Europe. Proud mother of two daughters and one grandson, Cher encourages them to pursue their dreams of no limits!

Follow her on social media (@cher_terais (all major platforms) @cher_terais_author on TikTok) to learn more about this amazing author who calls the suburbs of Atlanta home!

Don't forget to checkout other books in the Wanderlust Romance series!

Mess on the Mara

Tempest in Tulum

Stay even more connected by scanning the QR Code below to get bonus content for Cher Terais's books. Discover the fun things like:

The soundtrack to this book and the others

Inspiration boards and visuals for each book;

Free downloadables, short stories and more!

https://linktr.ee/Cher_Terais

The trip doesn't stop here! *The Booked Club* community and podcast are COMING SOON!

Sign up for my mailing list for more details!